THE ROCK OF THE MISSING

AF358542

Second AEINAPE prize for novels 2015

ANTONIO FLÓREZ LAGE

THE ROCK OF THE MISSING

Published in 2017

Depósito legal: GC 515-2017

ISBN: 978-84-697-3783-5

© Antonio Flórez Lage, 2017

Translation: Olga Núñez Miret

Editing: Wendy Janes

Book cover: Javier Ruiz León

Printed in Spain

Don't you dare think I don't know

who this isn't dedicated to

If I jump, I'll kill myself; if I don't jump, they'll kill me.

It's starting to rain. The heavy and huge drops falling intermittently seem to do it in slow-motion and are only the prelude to the huge thunderstorm that's about to break out. The wind dies and everything remains suspended in a strange calm, waiting for the demons to burst out.

I am naked, shivering from the cold; they are waiting impatiently behind me. I have to jump. I look at the sky and at the sea, everything is dark grey, it looks like a black and white movie. I close my eyes and the rest of my senses sharpen: I hear the waves breaking against the rock on top of which I am standing; I feel the raindrops tapping on my head and flooding me with a strong smell of wet soil. I have to jump. I start breathing more deeply; I will need a lot of oxygen. I take in as much air as I can and then I let it go slowly. It reminds me of my childhood, diving at the beach. The images of those summers flash quickly through my head and my friend is present in all of them. I am here because of him. What a friend! A whole life dedicated to his strange sense of humour. What an individual, peculiar, always getting me into trouble... I have to jump. I don't want to think of anything that might distract me.

I carry on breathing deeply with my eyes closed; I need to relax. I try to think of something that will motivate me. I remember the scene of the protagonists of *Chariots of Fire* running on the beach, with the spectacular soundtrack playing in the background. I cheer up and calm a bit. I visualise Paul Newman in *Cool Hand Luke,* convinced that he can eat fifty eggs. I can do it.

I open my eyes and look down, to the exact point my body must dive into. The height is very high, the tide is very low. I realise we're in September, the month of the strong tides. I hadn't thought about such things for a long time…

I'm going to jump.

I'm going to settle my score with the Rock of the Missing.

I inhale for the last time, fill my lungs up to bust and leap into the void.

Chapter 1. The peculiar friend and the mysterious rock

My friend was an extraordinary being from the very beginning: on receiving the time-tested slap to welcome him into the world, he laughed out loud. It was something unheard of, newborns don't laugh, they don't even smile, but that was a belly laugh, without a doubt. All who witnessed it have died since, but the story remains. That's what makes stories what they are: the way facts stand the reversals of time and death. The witness accounts remain when matter disappears.

He looked like a serious man, which was his greatest virtue. He had a strange sense of humour, all his own, that only he truly understood. When I saw him looking happy and I didn't know why, I guessed he had managed to carry out one of his challenges. He was born to laugh at the world. He was an adult playing a part in a theatrical comedy for little children. As it was a role that was neither serious nor real, he always played with gusto, fearlessly. He was forever trying to do funny things, testing himself with new challenges to avoid the boredom of always playing the same part, repetitive, simple and grey. If he didn't do that, it was all too easy and tedious.

He was born to a rich family with pedigree, in a fishing village. From very young he had to act before the public with the sense of responsibility of a man who knows much is expected of him: an appropriate behaviour, a smart dress, a public image, a know-how. He had to be an actor full-time; he spent his time studying how people act. By observing and analysing, he learned to interpret those small gestures that define you, give you away, and make you vulnerable. What each person does, why, the consequences of maintaining a posture. In sum, the things we show and the things we hide, the strong and the weak points of people. The washing we hang out for it to be seen, but also that humid and dirty cellar we hide, ashamed. All the things that betray us, accuse us and leave us exposed and naked in front of others.

His talent would have allowed him to become a millionaire, to be famous, a leader, a winner… However, he fled from all that. He thought it was peculiarly pathetic to be a leader or a millionaire in a theatrical comedy. Within a comedy, you can aspire to one thing and one thing only: to be funny. To try and induce a unique and special hilarity, to look for actions that will leave a small footprint for those who know how to appreciate them. The only indulgence he allowed himself, given his ability, was to manipulate the actors during the performance. He liked to turn the performance into something reasonably fair – according to his own criteria for justice, of course.

He wasn't a normal person, although he enjoyed boasting about it. Perhaps for him, reality was just that: to realise that nothing was serious or real.

I didn't always understand the way he behaved; I often judged him harshly. However, his teachings inspired me and have helped me be happier. What we shared, from the moment I met him until his death, marked me for life. A life, mine, linked forever to my peculiar friend and a mysterious rock: the Rock of the Missing.

The Rock of the Missing is a large boulder that protrudes from the sea around a hundred metres from the coast. Its black and threatening silhouette is drawn in outline over the sky from the nearby beach of the Drowned (Los Ahogados). You don't need to be very good at sports to get there swimming, if that's what you really want. A few ledges, like steep steps, help the climb to the top. This isn't the real problem either. Up there, there is a small platform, eight metres or so above the sea, which allows crazy, thoughtless or desperate people to get ready to jump. Looking down generates a titanic wrestling match between fear and vertigo, one paralyses you and the other pushes you to leap into the void. You feel a rush of adrenaline. You see several submerged rocks making a circle, a target you must hit. You must drop right in the centre of that kind of deep well if you want to avoid death. Once airborne, the fall seems to become eternal and it feels as if that feared crash will never come. Then, finally, you hit the sea surface and feel how you are sinking without bumping into anything hard. You've avoided the feared rocks and you are flooded very briefly by calm, but that false sense of calm flees like a flock of seagulls before a rabid dog when you notice the vacuum effect dragging you to the bottom. In that precise moment, you realise, terrified, that the legends are true.

All the stories about the underwater cavern underneath the Rock of the Missing were impressive. That, of course, fed the myth. The first strange event happened a long time ago. My grandmother told me the story, as her father had told her before. Some fishermen were coming back after spending the whole day at sea. They were three young men from the village, two brothers and their cousin, all around twenty years old, sons of fishermen, grandsons of fishermen: sea salt running through their veins. That day they had stayed longer, trying to increase their catch. The night was falling as they were making their way back on their boat and they decided to approach the Rock. Although it was late, there was a full moon and the sea was completely calm, therefore they didn't think there was any danger.

At the foot of the huge rock, there was a distinct and small well. Thanks to the low tide, the rocks were clearly visible, slightly above the surface. As they'd caught few fish, they still had bait left and they decided to throw their fishing tackle on that hole. The cousin anchored the boat and the two brothers jumped onto the rock circle. Perhaps they would be able to save the day at the last minute…

Everything happened very quickly. One of the brothers slipped and fell into the well, immediately disappearing. The other one dropped everything he was holding and jumped in after him without thinking about it. The third fisherman steered the boat closer and looked on, impotent. He circled that dark hole where his two cousins had disappeared, shouted out their names, but didn't dare to dive in. Finally, he submerged his head carefully, trying to see something. The water was quiet and dark, giving off a strong smell of fish. He stuck his head farther in and then he felt a force pulling him towards the deep. He fled, terrified.

That night only the traumatised cousin went back. All later searches were totally fruitless. They didn't find them, dead or alive. A little bit later, the cousin left the village and nobody heard about him again. In a way, he also disappeared.

Nobody ever came back. Years later, some would swear they had seen one of the brothers, looking very different, in a big city, but nobody could ever confirm that.

From that moment on, every ten or fifteen years the strange disappearances would happen again. Whether they were desperate suicidal people, thoughtless youths, daring adventurers or those chased during the Civil War, there was always some reckless individual who dove from the rock and disappeared forever. That meant that each subsequent generation had a disappearance more or less close in time, and the legend and the fear continued among the villagers.

To begin with, demons and gods were blamed for the disappearances; later on, people started to believe they didn't just vanish but reappeared in a different place or a different time. The underwater cavern changed them forever and they didn't want to, or couldn't, come back.

What really happened to those who dove under the Rock of the Missing?

Chapter 2. Mexico

"You must bite a hair of the dog that bit you yesterday," the waiter blurted out at me.

I was starting my August holiday and I had gone out the night before to celebrate. After getting up late with a mammoth hangover, a cold shower managed to wake me up enough to restore my humanity. I left the International House – the welcoming hostel where I was staying – with my head hung low and hair still wet. The bright sun and the bustle of some kids playing on the street hurt me so intensely that I had no option but to enter a nearby tavern all students avoided. It was totally empty, so I could choose the table farthest away from the painful light entering the windows and flooding the place. The plastic tablecloth, dirty and sticky, reminded me there was no room to be fussy. I began to feel irritated at my bad choice. I promised myself I would accept and resign myself to whatever came next to avoid the explosion of anger starting to build up inside of me. The waiter, guessing my hangover, approached me, kind and understanding.

"A coffee, please," I asked, rather curtly.

"If you got pissed in Mexico, you have to cure the hangover in true Mexican style: cold *chela* [beer] and very hot *chilaquiles* [fried crunchy bits of tortilla with chilli sauce]. My granddaddy used to say: 'You must bite a hair of the dog that bit you yesterday, that's how you get better.'"

I did not feel I could say no without losing my temper, and therefore I accepted.

While I waited for my *chilaquiles*, sipping tiny sips of a cold Sol beer, a bold man with a huge blond moustache entered the place. He was fat as a barrel and sweating buckets. The unbuttoned shirt and the disgusting shorts he was wearing couldn't accommodate a single wrinkle more. There was no doubt that he'd slept in the same clothes. He came straight to my table and sat down. Only once he had made himself comfortable did he bother to ask for my permission. Judging by his accent he seemed a foreigner, perhaps German.

"Does it bother you if we share a table?"

The waiter came back right then with my *chilaquiles* and he tried to help me.

"Crazy *pinche* philosopher, leave the foreigner alone. It's too early for your foolishness."

I looked at the waiter, who winked at me with a knowing expression; I looked around, taking in the rest of the empty tables. My hangover and my irritation had made my usual shyness disappear. I didn't want to behave too familiarly with him and tried to keep my distance.

"Sir, you can sit wherever you fancy," I replied, sternly.

"All right, my philosopher," the waiter intervened, derisively, after my conformity. "Busy today? What are you having?"

The other one didn't acknowledge the barb.

"My usual," he ordered, nonchalantly. "Do you know what the *valemadrismo* is?" he asked, staring at me while he lit a cigar.

I was eating and the cigar bothered me.

"I hope you won't mind that I eat while you smoke…" I said, ironically.

"Not at all, *güey*," he said, ignoring my dig.

After a long silence, he repeated the question.

"Do you know what the *valemadrismo* is?"

"*Me vale madre* means I don't care at all," I replied, irritated.

"More or less. I'll explain it better to you: *valemadrista* is the person who lives according to the theory of the *valemadrismo*. The said theory implies that you don't care for anything, that everything is the same to you. A good *valemadrista* is usually a *huevón*. *Huevón* is a guy who lives the *hueva*. It's difficult to define the *hueva*. You must try to think of the highest degree of laziness ever experienced, then you take it to the nth degree and you'll only be scratching the surface of that deep feeling. The most important thing in life is to be *valemadrista*, even beyond being a *huevón*. There is a big interconnection between both trends, but while the *valemadrismo* is pure philosophy, being a *huevón* is an addendum or a consequence, although it's truly fundamental. You'll only be a good *huevón* if you don't care at all about the consequences of your *hueva*..."

Right then I could no longer contain the violence I'd been holding back all morning. The fury took over my body and, while I screamed at him with my face turning bright red, I stood up so suddenly that the chair fell to the floor.

"Go to hell! You're a bore!"

I left the bloody place grumbling and I heard somebody calling my name. It took me a bit of time to know who the young guy who was approaching me with a smile was. He'd changed a bit and I didn't expect to see him there. To find a person from a small Galician village in the middle of a big Mexican city was baffling, but the fact that he was my friend, was even more so. I had an initial bittersweet feeling that left me somewhat paralysed. After spending many summers together, we argued precisely on the last day and the punch I gave him ended my childhood holidays on a sad note. I never set foot again in that pretty village and that punch became our goodbye.

Without hesitating, he gave me a hug as soon as he saw me.

"It's been such a long time! What are you doing here?"

"Eh… I have a scholarship. Eh… And you?"

"A business trip. My company has businesses to attend to here. They wanted to send somebody well-trained, serious and experienced, but they didn't have anybody, and here I am." He laughed, amused. "The meeting is this afternoon; afterwards I'll take some time off to travel and get to know the country. Do you know Mexico well?"

"Eh… Not that much. I haven't had time to travel. I've just started the holidays…"

"I'm hungry," he interrupted me. "Follow me."

He took me around the block to a taco place. The small greasy truck where they served them gave off an abundant and tasty aroma. We moved slowly forward among the numerous clients besieging the place. He asked for two *tacos al pastor* [tacos shepherd style]. I didn't want to eat mine and he devoured both. When he finished, he produced a toothpick and put it in his mouth.

"Now you use a toothpick?" I asked, on observing that detail. "It doesn't befit at all somebody with your fine education."

"Show it some respect. It's a cocktail stick. And you must call it Mr Cocktail Stick."

He ordered a couple of beers – "a couple of *chelas*" was what he said. He ostentatiously raised his little finger when drinking. I found his affectation funny again, but this time I said nothing. To break the silence, I got talking about the Galician village where we used to spend our summer holidays as kids. It was a bond that connected us and I still had an unanswered question that tortured me.

"What do you know about the village?" I asked him.

"Same as usual… Ah, no!" he said, completely changing his facial expression. "What a blunder!

Everything has changed. They've installed a set of traffic lights!"

"Traffic lights?"

"Yes, traffic lights. Technology and urbanism have finally reached the Galician hamlet. The brightness brought on by the traffic lights is the symbol of the illumination putting an end to centuries of obscurantism. No expenses have been spared. Now the traffic is much more fluid. The endless traffic jams of a hamlet with four cars are finished. You must see it!"

"Where have they installed it?" I asked, smiling.

"In the middle of the village, right next to *El Corte Inglés* [a well-known chain of Spanish department stores]…"

"*El Corte Inglés*? You are joking, right?"

"Yes, of course, we haven't got that far." He laughed. "But haven't you ever thought that having a branch of *El Corte Inglés* is what determines that a big village or a town has turned into a city? If you have one it gives you cachet as an urban area, it gives you stature and class."

"Do you remember the beach crabs?" I interrupted him, steering the conversation in the direction I wanted.

"Of course I remember them! I was the one who taught you how to catch them!" he objected, looking very serious.

"Come on, man!"

"Are you sure?" he insisted, with a joking expression.

"Ha, ha, ha. What do you know about the people there? Have you heard anything from Pirulo?" Pirulo was the idol of our teenage years, the village's paradigm, the last rebel, the king of the mad ones.

"Pirulo carries on the same; he's made a pact with the devil. I swear to you he'll never die."

"He'll bury us all…"

"Without a doubt," he asserted, laughing.

"Did they discover anything else out about Bad Quique?" I asked, finally confronting what I really wanted to know, while a wave of panic overtook me and made me feel like a child again.

"No. The one who disappeared was Don Prudencio. Do you remember him? One day they found his boat broken and empty. In point of fact, it was close to the Rock of the Missing," he said, deliberately. "It was lodged between some rocks, that was why it didn't sink and they managed to find it. Don Prudencio wasn't inside; they didn't find him. People say that when he realised he could no longer look after himself, he tied a basket full of stones to his ankle and he jumped into the sea, and that was why they never found him. Others think he went diving under the Rock of the Missing, you can imagine… I believe that theory. Do you remember what he told us?"

"Damn village full of crazy people and weird mysteries," I swore, trying to pretend calm and aplomb. "A long time has gone by, but I still remember it as if branded by fire. It's as if that good man, Don Prudencio, was telling us the story right now. That summer has been branded into my brain in such way that I remember it all precisely and in detail. As if one could ever forget such a thing…”

My friend nodded and didn’t add anything else. I had noticed a special shine in his eyes when he talked about the Rock of the Missing; afterwards, he’d gone quiet and thoughtful.

“I only invest in forgetting,” he mumbled as he ordered another beer.

He took a sip, looked at his watch and paid the bill.

“I’m sorry; I’m in a bit of a hurry. I must go to a meeting so boring that I feel like inviting you to it.”

I laughed. Truly, he hadn’t changed at all.

“Hey, don’t laugh,” he protested, smiling, while he changed his expression to one of fake annoyance, “I still owe you a punch, you thug. I haven’t forgotten it.”

Before I had a chance to apologise, he spoke again.

“I’ll come to fetch you tonight and we’ll go to have some tacos and beers. Where are you staying?”

“At the International House, a hostel in Alemania Street. Do you know where it is?”

“I’ll find it, don’t worry. I’ll pick you up at nine o’clock.”

Nothing predicted I’d end up going to sleep frightened to death, with a knife under my bed that same night.

Chapter 3. Dark Shadow

In a small fishing village in Galicia was where I learned those necessary things that go beyond books. In those intense summers, my life filled up with colour and adventures. I was a city boy and was fascinated by everything related to nature. The sea exerted upon me a hypnotic and addictive effect, hijacking and monopolising all my thoughts. With the picture of the future catch in my head, I ruminated happily about what the day would bring. An infinity of fascinating and unknown species hid under those mysterious waters.

In the sunny mornings of low tides and crystalline waters, it was impossible to conceive of a better place to go crabbing. With my trident and a couple of bags to put the catch in, I ran to the beach with the sense of urgency of somebody who believes that the day flies with each single passing second. When I got there, I entered the water to where it reached my waist and I walked up and down the shore.

With the crabs, I followed three rules: to never catch females with eggs, to never catch small crabs and to always seek as fair a fight as possible. I enjoyed giving them a chance to defend themselves and escape; therefore I used only my naked hand – it wasn't fair to use the trident for assistance. I enjoyed, in particular, the ones that put up a fight and raised their claws to defend themselves.

Nobody ever wanted to come with me, so I got used to going alone. Epic fights replayed themselves in my imagination during those long walks, and after mythological battles I was able to defeat those strange and enormous beings. The truly great thing is that, sometimes, something similar really took place, and I would catch a giant spider crab. Then I'd go back home happy, imagining the faces of my parents when they saw my catch. They'd be truly impressed and proud.

I was on my way back from the beach with my bag full of crabs and I realised I was being followed. I turned around and saw him. He was wearing dark blue swimming trunks – he always wore the same colour trunks – a white T-shirt and his red cap full of badges. Hair blond, skin white, skinny and sinewy. A pretty normal appearance, nothing too noticeable, except for the badges. Seated on his shiny red BH bicycle, he was pedalling very slowly, almost keeping pace with me, and he was staring at me intensely. That is the first image I have of him. I remember it with total clarity because he looked at me for a long time, openly. I was shy and he must have realised straight away.

"Can you show me what you're carrying in the bag?" he finally asked me, kindly.

I didn't fancy showing him my catch, but I didn't know how to say no.

"They are very small."

His statement, hurtful and unnecessary, irked me. Usually, I wouldn't have replied, but the impertinence of having stared at me for so long, only to then come out with such nonsense, smashed through the barrier of frustrating self-restraint my shyness enforced upon me. I felt my blood boil.

"Like your balls, asshole!"

Then, he came out with one of his usual retorts. He laughed good-humouredly, composed a humble and conciliatory expression and told me:

"Good reply. You've been very quick. Forgive me; I was pulling your leg. Would you mind teaching me how to catch them? I'd like to go with you."

His retreat made me feel shy again. Red like a beetroot, I nodded and stuttered:

"Well, OK."

And that was how we started to go fishing for crabs together. After spending the whole summer catching them on the beach, it was on a hot September day when everything started to get complicated.

In the area of Galicia where we spent our summer holidays, the strong September tides are known as *lagarteiras*. Every year around that time, the tide would rise and fall more than usual and everything became magical. It was when the strangest things happened and when I was more eager than usual to go to the beach. During those mysterious days, the low tide allowed us access to places normally unreachable and offered us treasures hidden the rest of the year.

That day I had got up so early that, when I arrived at the beach, my friend wasn't there yet. The tide had fallen and had nearly reached the area where the fishing boats were moored. The sea felt eerie, but at first, I couldn't work out why. After a while, I realised no crabs were visible, and that disconcerting emptiness was what didn't fit in. I decided to try farther in, to see if I was lucky that way. The water already reached above my belly button.

At first I thought they were shreds of nets some boat had lost. The fishes would have got caught in them, attracting other fishes and crabs. I approached carefully, very slowly. The water almost reached my chest and I had difficulty moving.

To see what was underneath, the only thing I could do was dive. I breathed in deeply several times, accumulated as much air as I could and dove into the freezing water. Only then did I realise what they were: fishing traps. Traps full of beach crabs, velvet crabs and spider crabs! I didn't expect to see them in that banned area. Whoever had placed them there was breaking the law and risking a big fine. I got worked up; I could get myself into trouble. I was thinking about it when I saw my friend approaching. Anxious to share my fears, I rushed to him and told him everything.

"Perfect," he cheered mischievously. "Imagine what we'll do…"

"I wouldn't report it. If we grass them up, the owner of the traps will have to pay a big fine. And he'll kill us for sure."

"We aren't going to report anybody, man! What we're going to do is keep what's inside the traps. There's nobody around."

I looked at him, afraid.

"There's nobody close enough to observe if we're getting the crabs out of the sand or from the traps," he insisted.

The idea of getting hold of those crabs was tempting, but I remained fearful.

"Let's get all the crabs out. We'll only keep the biggest and we'll set the rest free," he insisted again.

Finally, I agreed. They were doing something illegal, depleting my beach and my crabs. What the fuck! They deserved a little punishment.

Both of us swam under at the same time, grabbed the first trap and pulled it hard to drag it to the shore. It wasn't very heavy, but the rope tied to the rest of the traps worked as ballast and it was impossible to move. Exhausted after several attempts, we had to rethink our method. That trap wasn't very deep, but we were diving again and again with little rest. The repeated effort under the water had left us exhausted.

"We won't move them like that," I said, breathless.

"You're right. We must hurry; the tide is starting to rise."

He decided that the best way wasn't to move the traps, but for us to move. Go from trap to trap, getting the crabs out. The problem was that, although the first trap was close to the shore, the rest were in deeper water. Also, with the rising tide, the depth was increasing.

Usually, the traps opened on one side, by untying a knot. That allowed for the easy removal of its content. However, in our case, it wasn't possible to untie the knots under the water. The only option was to insert the hand through the tube the crabs used to enter and extract them through there. To blindly introduce our little hands and try different positions to get hold of them was mad. If they grabbed a finger with their claws, the pain would be unbearable. A big crab could cut you badly, and a big edible crab would smash the finger to bits.

"I'm not going to put my hand in there. It's madness," I protested.

"Follow me."

Once he made up his mind, he acted quickly and decidedly. Either you joined him or you were left on your own, he gave you no option. As usual, I joined him.

The first trap was easy, for the second we had to dive deeper. He dove in with energy, put his hand inside the trap and got a huge spider crab out.

"You're mad as a hatter. If it catches one of your fingers, it will wreck it," I said, shaking my head.

We repeated the operation from trap to trap, from crab to crab. We got so many that they didn't fit inside the bags and we had to let many of them go, keeping only the largest ones.

When we reached the last trap, we saw it was secured to the anchor of the boat belonging to Dark Shadow, an individual hated and feared in the village. The idea was good; when the time to collect them came, it would be an easy task: raise the anchor and pull the rope all the traps hung from.

The last trap, the one closest to the boat, was quite deep.

"I'm very tired. It's your turn," he ordered me.

Although I was very scared, I didn't dare refuse; we were supposed to share the catch. I gave him the bags with the crabs, closed my eyes and inhaled deeply several times. I positioned myself right on the vertical line above the trap and dove with strong arm movements. I looked through the net to try and see what was inside, but I had no air left and could only see a huge shape before I had to come up for air.

"Coward!"

"I only wanted to know what I'm going to find inside. One has to look before putting the hand in. I haven't even tried it yet," I objected, stung.

I breathed in again and dove towards the trap. When I got there, I put my hand inside the entry tube and moved it with caution, from side to side. Finally, I touched something very big. Judging by the rough feel it seemed a spider crab. I tried to grab it by its shell, but I couldn't. It was moving a lot. Then, I managed to grab two of its legs and I pulled hard. I didn't have much air left and my only concern was to get it out and reach the surface. I shook it hard and managed to dislodge it. The journey back from the deep seemed to last forever; I thought I wouldn't make it, but for some reason, I didn't let go of the creature. Once out, I breathed in, feeling a combination of anguish and liberation, and relinquished the spider crab.

"Well done," he shouted while he grabbed it from me. "This is the biggest of all the ones we've caught. See? It wasn't so hard!"

I'd managed! Euphoric with the adrenaline rush after the accumulated tension, I believed I was an exceptional and invincible being, a true hero.

Once on the shore, we shared the crabs. I kept my huge spider crab and went home, proud of my exploits. That evening, we ate a good seafood feast. The only thing that bothered me was not having said anything about the traps. Although I didn't really lie: I said I had caught them thanks to how low the tide was because of the *lagarteiras*…

The problem was that Dark Shadow, the man who'd planted the illegal traps, had seen us dive close to his boat, and when he collected the empty traps, he guessed what we'd done.

Dark Shadow was a sullen and violent man, hated and feared in equal measure by the villagers. His nickname came from his quiet and quick skill for robbing and committing crimes. He had placed some traps in an illegal area, but that wasn't his most serious crime, not by a long chalk. Everything he had, he had obtained by robbing others or doing bad things.

He had a famous house in the mountains, close to the cliffs. It was built in an illegal place, but the mayor had turned a blind eye and nobody had dared to confront him. The water for the house came from a nearby stream, and he stole it by diverting the course of the stream and leaving the rest of the people with no water. He then denied everything, and because up there, in the mountains, he lived alone, it was impossible to catch him red-handed. He had also planted several areas of the mount with eucalyptus trees. They weren't his, but when the owner died, he took over the plots. The rightful heirs lived in big cities and didn't want to go to court; it was too complicated for people who didn't live there. Not happy with that, the size of his eucalyptus plantations kept growing. In the Galician mountains, plots are delimited by *marcos*. The *marcos* are semi-buried stones, placed on the corners of the plots of lands, used to mark their boundaries. Every time he had a chance, he moved those stones a few metres, increasing his plot and planting a new row of eucalyptus on his property. Dark Shadow pruned his mount plots at the same time as the neighbours did. Once they were all cut down to size and planted at the same time, the size of the eucalyptus trees was the same and it was easier to include new rows of eucalyptus of the same size that went unnoticed. That way, the small mountain plots kept growing.

During the last couple of years, the price of wood had increased and many had chopped down their mountain plots. Dark Shadow, of course, had also cut them down. With the money he'd earned, he decided to buy a bull: a prize stud bull he'd brought from afar. When we stole the crabs he'd just bought it. It had cost him a lot of money and he was planning on making tonnes of money by charging for mating the valuable animal. He was so proud of his animal that he built a good stable for it, in a plot close to his disturbing and enigmatic house. The house everybody talked about but inside of which nobody had ever set foot. It was surrounded by a fence with thick and thorny bushes that gave it a hostile appearance. To make it even more intimidating, there was an old and dirty sign at the entry, on a eucalyptus stick. The sign looked as if it had been written using a finger dipped in blood. Its lettering, rough and irregular, only said: "THINK ABOUT IT".

Think about it: that was Dark Shadow's threat. A sinister threat. Think about it. It didn't say anything, but it made you think. Think about it. Indeed it made one think.

Chapter 4. Peyote Man

There are times when, on looking back at the past, it's easy to correlate the facts and know how a story began, what was the origin of everything that came to pass later. Unfortunately, in that moment, when you're living through it, you don't realise that. What will end up changing our fate doesn't usually originate in something big, but in the most trivial way. The little details end up precipitating serious consequences that make our life change forever. Afterwards, when some time has passed, you might find the source, but not the logic of it. Some people try to extract a lesson or to point out where the mistake was, but those types of things are only nonsense; it's impossible to predict what will be the long-term results of every little decision we take. What I'm trying to convey with all this is that meeting the Peyote Man was the trigger for everything that happened to us later.

My friend came to pick me up at the agreed time. After an abundant dinner at a small taco place where he took me – he seemed to be an expert on those sorts of place – we went to a nearby canteen. There we did one of the things that can be most thrilling for a man: drinking with a childhood friend. Talking about one's memories and the feats of one's youth provides us with unrivalled pleasure. The words flew as fast as the beer bottles, in an unstoppable spiral. Time ran at that great speed it only reaches on nights of revelry and with us hardly noticing it was closing time. While they put everything away, they allowed us to have the last one. Apart from the waiters, we were the only ones left with another lonesome patron: a guy who looked like a hippy and was drinking on the corner of the bar. At a given moment he joined us. He had a South-American accent, although we couldn't work out exactly where from.

The Peyote Man wore trousers made of very thin material, old and threadbare, and a T-shirt nearly transparent, so worn it was. He had some kind of scarf around his neck, also very worn. There were no colours: all his clothing was of a uniform colour, sun-bleached. The trousers might have been green a long time ago; the T-shirt might have been beige; the scarf might have been orange, or not. His footwear was the most striking thing of all: a very peculiar pair of flip-flops with a piece of tyre in place of a sole.

He was neither young nor old; it was difficult to be precise about his age. He had a long and dirty beard, and his hair wasn't far behind. Tall and thin, very tanned, his skin was blackened by the sun. What was really scary was his gaze. Underneath thick black eyebrows hid two light blue eyes, of the lightest blue, that looked as if they had also been sun-bleached. They were lively eyes, and they conferred a special intensity to his gaze. A slight madness peered threat-eningly through that gaze, and it was even more evident once he started talking.

"I like to drink," he blurted out, looking possessed. "It's good for the mind."

"To drinking!" my friend shouted.

We burst out laughing, toasted and drank a big gulp of our beers.

"I'm going to explain a curious theory to you," my friend said. "The Theory of the Big Louse. According to that theory, it's not necessary to wash your hair every day, far from it. I try not to wash it; I see you do the same," he said, addressing the Peyote Man. "When you don't wash your hair, the lice start to feel comfortable; they grow and reproduce in their natural habitat. There are more and more of them and the process of competitiveness and natural selection starts. They are crowded and start to die. Some die of illness, others kill each other... There comes a time when there's only one survivor: the Big Louse. It has killed the rest; it's managed to become bigger and stronger than the rest. It's so big that you can easily see it, so you grab it with two fingers; you remove it and throw it on the fire. At that precise moment, your head is clean, no louse. If you can be patient, and wait for that moment, you'll discover that shampoo is not necessary."

We laughed again – waiters, who had come closer to listen to the story, included. Afterwards, that strange individual with dirty hair was silent, thinking.

"Have you tried peyote?" he asked us, suddenly.

We shook our heads negatively.

"You can't leave without trying peyote. You must go to the desert and try it. It will change your lives."

"How?" my friend asked, very interested.

"It changes everything. I went to the desert looking for peyote. It's a small cactus that hardly protrudes from the soil. The right person must help you find it... I tried it once and I repeated. I spent three months taking it and my life changed forever. I now look at the world through that experience. I look at the people who haven't lived what I have and I laugh; they don't know what I know... I do! I asked questions and found answers. I discovered the secret. When I went back to my country, I had changed a lot. My interaction with the people I knew was different. Some I didn't like before, now I liked; others I'd liked in the past, I no longer cared for. They didn't understand it, didn't know why... But I did!"

On saying that, his eyes shone with a special light, even crazier if that was at all possible. His lips trembled and saliva accumulated in the corners of his mouth. He laughed very loudly, with a demented and weird laughter.

"Now I can see people's auras," he continued. "The connections that link each person with the rest and with nature. You are hiding something," he said, looking at my friend. "I see something weird in you, something bad you don't want to show. It hurts you; I can see it in your aura. You're sick."

"Yes, it's true," he agreed, very serious. "My aura has something very bad I've been trying to hide all night: I'm suffering diarrhoea."

I managed to hold back my laughter. The Peyote Man ignored the comment. He was too involved in his own speech. He carried on talking.

"When you are under the influence of peyote don't waste any time, you must mentally approach Mezcalito. Look for him, he's the oracle, he's the one you must ask questions about yourselves, about your lives. He'll answer, but you must ask him the right questions. Go to a small village close to Real de Catorce; it's called San Antonio de Coronados. Ask for Doña Toña; tell her I sent you, Peter Marco. She'll help you."

"Is Mezcalito the true prince of the Green Beings?" my friend asked, winking at me.

"That's not important; he's the one who solves our doubts and that's it. Don't play with me; remember that I can see your games."

"We must consult him about our deepest doubts," I suggested.

"That's it. You have truly understood it," he asserted. "Tell Doña Toña I sent you, Peter Marco. She lives in a house next to the church, don't forget. Remember Doña Toña, Doña Toña… You must ask for Doña Toña, bloody ignorant shit-eaters… Excuse me, did I just think that last bit or did I say it out loud?" he asked, looking surprised.

We didn't even have a chance to answer. He stood up and started rummaging around his pocket, but my friend was faster.

"We'll get this. Thanks for your wonderful advice."

Peyote Man thanked him with a courteous nod. He got to the door walking fast, and nimbly flipped the latch and got lost in the dark night.

6:58 a.m. (still drunk)

The night had been intense. It had started at the taco stand, had carried on at the canteen and finally, it had taken us to the elite night club Pachito Pupupi, from where we'd been thrown out at closing time. Beer and tequila gave name and surname to that night of excesses. My friend was sharing with me one of his peculiar theories.

"I'm going to tell you something funny related to the tricks used to confound people during negotiations: the Triple Negation. Two negations become an affirmation. For example, if you tell me: 'Don't say no,' what you want me to say is yes. If you say: 'I don't want to deny it,' what you're doing is asserting it. The two negations annul each other. If you push those kinds of sentences it helps confound matters: 'I don't want you not to go.' But it's possible to give another turn to the screw, and that's how we reach the Triple Negation. If we include a third negation in the sentence it increases the difficulty in comprehension."

"Three negations? How?"

"Don't think I don't know it's not easy."

"You're crazy!"

"I don't think you don't know it's not true."

While we were laughing, we saw a beautiful Mexican woman approaching us. She smiled and her huge enigmatic eyes sparkled.

"Good morning. We haven't had breakfast yet. Don't tell us you're not coming to eat something with us because you're not hungry," I blurted, the alcohol making me feel brave, and I pointed at a nearby taco stand.

"You're from Spain, aren't you? I like how you talk, it sounds very cool."

My friend said goodbye, after eating his second taco and took a third for the way. I stayed with the gorgeous Mexican woman and we talked for a long time. She told me she was a painter. The subject offered lots of scope and I asked her quite a few questions. In the end, she invited me to her house to show me her paintings. I looked her in the eye and her pretty smile totally won me over.

We entered her house, went to her bedroom and she kissed me. It was a hot and wet kiss. She jumped on me pushing me backwards. The bedroom door closed due to our impetus. I grabbed her lustily and pressed her to my body. We then heard a knock and we stopped kissing; somebody was pushing the door from the other side. Luckily, we were leaning on it and they couldn't open it. We stayed motionless, preventing the entry of whoever was pushing from outside.

A voice sounded, evidently angry.

"Zulema?"

She moved away and opened the door. A young man, a bit older than me, appeared.

"Eh… Hi, Alejandro," she stuttered trying to cover it up. "Eh… I'm showing my drawings to a Spanish art student. He was telling me I might be able to have an exhibition in Spain. This is Alejandro, my boy-friend," she introduced us.

The boy looked at each of us in turn with hatred in his face: first, he looked at me, then at her. I offered him my hand, baffled still. My face must have been a picture. He didn't even blink. He stared at Zule with violence and she lowered her head. Then he turned towards me and made as if to punch me. I moved away, afraid. Then he laughed angrily, turned around and left the room.

"See you later!" was his threatening goodbye, before leaving the house, banging the door loudly.

I observed Zule for a little while. She was very frightened. I offered to keep her company, but she refused. I insisted and she got very anxious, so I said goodbye, kissing her clumsily on the face.

When I crossed the threshold I felt scared. Would that madman be waiting for me? Filled with suspicion, I looked to both sides, and ran away. After running for a few minutes, I felt breathless and started to walk. It took me a good while to get to the International House. I entered, crestfallen, brooding; I was feeling sad and tired. I wanted to see that girl again, but I shouldn't do it. I didn't know her boyfriend and he seemed very violent. It wouldn't be difficult for him to find out where I was staying; I recalled I had told Zule. I got scared, convinced that he'd come to find me.

When I got to my room I locked the door carefully, I wedged a chair on the door and hid a big kitchen knife right under my bed.

Chapter 5. The Ghost Yacht

In a sombre fishing village where darkness reigns unchecked under perpetual grey storm clouds, where rain and wind aren't the exceptions but the norm and the thick mantle of fog hides things you don't want to imagine, most of us were superstitious. Fears grow wings to fly into the homes and claws with which to clutch onto the souls of the fearful.

To be at the mercy of each push of the sea makes you conscious of how tiny and fragile you are and drives you to believe that if you follow certain rules you'll survive. That's how one starts to read signals where there aren't any because nothing is easier than seeing what one wishes to. Some would not go out to sea certain days; others would only sail out after passing with their boat three times below a small chapel up on the cliffs... They all had their ghosts and their rituals.

The story of the ghost yacht spread through the village quickly: a French yacht and its crew had disappeared.

The last ones to see it had been some fishermen. It was anchored near the coast. Then a storm arrived. A huge thunderstorm lashed the village. Only the oldest inhabitants could remember something similar. The unleashed wind and the choppy water furiously hit the windows, which hardly managed to resist the enraged onslaught of nature. Thunder and lightning thrashed the river, generating a terrifying uproar. The waves swept the whole beach, mercilessly whipping the houses closest to the coast. All forces of nature battled without quarter to prove which one was the most powerful.

Once the thunderstorm had ended, the assessment of the damages followed. The village and its surrounding areas showed a Dantesque appearance. Upside-down boats or severely damaged vessels could be seen all over the estuary. It was as if a giant had ruthlessly gone stomping around a bathtub full of toys. Some boats, impelled by the storm, piled up, smashed to bits, over the beach. Barges were found in the most unexpected places, even deep inland. The houses had also suffered their toll; many looked beat-up, dirty, wounded, showing the horrendous scars from such a brutal fight. Huge numbers of trees had been knocked down or split in two, and their large trunks lay on the floor flat and unburied. But, although it might be difficult to believe, there were no victims in the village. We had all taken cover; the old fishermen had warned us well in advance.

Over the following days, the victims of the storm landed on the beach: trunks, the bodies of seabirds, huge shells, wooden planks, weird conches... Were the treasures the sea offered a redress for the harm caused or was it only returning what didn't belong to it? One morning, a French flag appeared on the beach. Then, the sailors remembered the yacht from before the storm that nobody had seen since. They informed the nearby villages. Nothing. Had it been sunk by the storm or had it been hijacked by ghosts or demons? It never turned up again, neither the vessel nor its crew. And that was what gave origin to the legend of the ghost yacht that had the whole village talking in those days.

My friend told me the story of the yacht and insisted we should go searching for the wreck.

"There's a cliff that has a hidden and difficult path to descend to the sea. Hardly anybody knows about it… We can go there, and we'll be able to see it all up close. Can you imagine if we managed to find the ghost yacht?"

"Don't you think the fishermen would have seen it already?" I replied, sceptical.

"The cliff is just at a point where the coast goes inland, leaving a tiny entry. In that area, there are strong currents and big rocks, therefore the fishermen never risk getting too close to it. Perhaps the currents will have dragged the yacht there."

"That's ridiculous. The coast is huge. Why should it be precisely there?"

"Because it hasn't been found yet and nobody has gone looking for it there. From a boat, it's too dangerous and not many people know about the path to climb down on foot. In winter, the currents empty the beach of its sand, leaving only the rocks and a few pebbles. However, when the tide is low, and only in the summer, there's a tiny beach left. It's a gorgeous virgin beach; we'll have a swim in an incredible place. Don't you fancy discovering a new beach?"

Seduced and encouraged by the opportunity of discovering a hidden place on that coast I thought I knew so well, I finally agreed, but without any conviction that we'd find the yacht.

We planned the excursion for the following day, calculating the time to set off in order to arrive at the beach at low tide. My friend was enthusiastic, with his usual cheerfulness and resolution. I was anxious.

We cycled to the point where the only bridle path ended. When he started walking down the pebble path that I knew ended at the house of Dark Shadow, I became alarmed. We usually didn't go near that place because the house, with its threatening sign, was scary. On that occasion, shortly after having stolen the crabs from his traps, I was horrified.

"What the fuck are we doing here?" I asked, terrified. "I hope you're not planning one of your tricks… I don't find it funny at all."

"Don't be a scaredy-cat," he replied, laughing. "I promise you I haven't any funny tricks planned against Dark Shadow. It's only a matter of climbing down to the beach. The path to descend the cliff is right behind his house. It's a coincidence. What can I do about it? Should I move the cliff? Anyway, he knows nothing about the crab traps; he has nothing against us."

I didn't want to talk about it anymore; we were close to his house already and he might hear us. I simply walked behind him, attentive to any noises.

We walked around the house and reached a humid forest of eucalyptus. At the end of the forest a ticket of furzes, over six feet high, blocked our way, the last barrier before reaching the cliff. Crossing it was impossible; the bushes were enormous, full of thorns and so thick that they created an insurmountable wall. There didn't seem to be any way to get through, but in between the maze created by the furzes, there was some sort of hidden path, serpentine and narrow, that allowed people to get through. My friend guided me behind a certain rock; the path started right there. It didn't look like a real path, only a small entry without an exit. I got scared.

"Where are you taking me? This doesn't seem to have an exit."

"Stop finding fault with everything. It has an exit. I've been there before. It keeps from one year to the next. It seems to be a route the wild animals use to cross."

"How do you know this path?"

A smile was his only and enigmatic reply.

We walked through the maze of furzes. It was possible to do it, but not without ending up with our arms and legs covered in scratches. It was the price we had to pay to reach the unknown. Once we came out of the path, he marked the place with a plastic bag tied to a furze.

"On the other side I use the rock to orient myself, but here there isn't anything. When one comes back and climbs up from the bottom of the cliff, it's not possible to find the entry point. That's why I always mark it with a plastic bag..."

Even after overcoming the barrier of furzes, it wasn't plain sailing. We had to go down a steep slope, weaving through rocks for almost an hour. We climbed down there slowly, careful not to slip. A small misstep and we would have rolled down to the bottom of the cliff.

When we finally got down, we were sweaty and exhausted. There was a small sandy area, surrounded by vast rocks, where we left our rucksacks. We took our T-shirts and sneakers off and steered straight to the water. We entered carefully; the waves crashed hard against the shore. The wounds caused by the furzes itched with the salt, but we dove happily into the freezing water.

"Be careful," he warned me. "The tide is going down and it pulls you in. Here the currents are very strong, don't go in too deep."

"Don't worry, I've already noticed that."

When we finished swimming, we lay on the sand to get warm. We unpacked our sandwiches and the water canteens, and we ate it all in a few minutes. We used our rucksacks as pillows to be more comfortable. With the heat of the sun and our full bellies, we quickly fell asleep.

We woke up drenched in sweat. We drank a bit of water and walked to the sea. We had to walk a bit to reach the shore; the tide was lower still and the beach had grown larger. When we reached the water, we saw a pole sticking out of the water in one of the corners of the beach. It was the area where the biggest rocks were. It hardly protruded from the surface, but it could be clearly seen.

"It's a boat's mast!" he shouted. "We've found the ghost yacht!"

I trained my eyes on it, becoming distracted for a moment, and he was already on his way towards the part of the beach closest to that mast.

"Follow me. We'll see it better from here," he shouted at me while climbing a big rock that was there.

We climbed onto the rock and we couldn't see anything. The sea crashed hard upon the shore. The foam and the turbulent water didn't allow us to see what was underneath.

"We must get closer to see what is there."

"You're mad! It's impossible to get in. If you go in, you'll drown. The waves will smash you against the rocks. You have already warned me about how strong the current is here."

"Don't worry. I'm a good swimmer. And, we're going to do one thing: I'll tie this rope to my waist," he said, taking out a long coiled rope.

"What are you doing with such a thing in your rucksack?"

"I had brought it to see if we could find some barnacles. I was planning on climbing down from those rocks to reach them; there are quite a few in that area."

"Don't fuck with me! You're mad!"

"That's why I hadn't told you anything. I didn't want to have to listen to you crying like a little girl."

"I think even that is a better idea than tying yourself up to go swimming… And I don't cry; I just love my life too much."

"Whatever you say, but I'm going to do it, with or without your help."

He began to tie the rope around his waist. I watched him silently, thinking about what chances he'd have if things got difficult. I knew I wouldn't convince him not to do it; therefore, I had to make sure there was as little danger as possible. I checked his knot; it was a good sailor's knot, it wouldn't untie. We tied the other end to a rock very close to the sea, another good knot. I looked him in the face: his expression was determined; he looked self-assured and focused.

"We'll see each other on the other side," he said as a goodbye, very serious.

"Don't be a jackass. It isn't funny."

He gave me the coiled rope and entered the water, laughing. The die was cast.

His strokes were elegant, professional. He lifted his head every so often to make sure he was going in the right direction. The distance was short, but he corrected his course constantly; the current was very strong. I tried to help him, unrolling the rope quickly as he advanced. Finally, he reached the mast and got hold of it while he had a rest. The position was uncomfortable: the waves rose and fell hard; the rope, tensed by the current, pulled him.

Suddenly, I no longer saw him.

No trace. Only waves and foam.

An overwhelming anxiety seized me.

Chapter 6. The Trip

I was having a few beers with Antonio, the concierge of the International House. We were sitting in the spacious hall of the hostel, talking animatedly. He was a very fat guy, dark haired and with a moustache; he had the looks and the face of the typical Mexican stereotype, the one who would appear in any advert. He was a joker, and he liked to pull my leg; he taught me puns and he would laugh at me because I didn't understand them. Good old Antonio worked as a concierge at night and as a chauffeur during the day and on the weekends. He didn't have a driving licence, but, as he said, he'd been driving his car since he was thirteen. The truth is that his old dented and clapped-out car always looked as if it was about to collapse.

My friend appeared and, when he saw we were drinking, he went to get more beers. I hadn't heard from him since the night when we'd gone out together. I hadn't heard anything about Zule or her boyfriend either; I had spent several days hardly going out of the International House.

When he arrived with the beers, we sat to chat and the first thing he did was ask me about the Mexican woman. I didn't wish to tell them what had happened and I brought up the matter of the peyote to change the subject; my friend loved those kinds of things. Then, we told Antonio what that crazy man had told us.

"The Peyote Man called me sick, that's very serious. A mentally ill person, because that guy had totally lost his mind, calling me crazy is something very funny. I compare it to the time when Pirulo called me crazy. You remember the chat with Pirulo, don't you? It seems that the nutters have got my number," he said, laughing.

"How could I not remember?" I replied, anguished when I remembered the ghosts of my childhood.

"I've completed the business deals that brought me here and have almost a month's holiday. I'm determined," he declared, looking convinced and dignified, "I'm going to San Antonio de Coronados, to Real de Catorce. I want to travel around Mexico and that will be my first destination. Are you in?"

I thought it was a fantastic idea. Distancing myself from Zule and her boyfriend was the best way to avoid problems. Travelling offered me an opportunity to escape and to let some time pass so that everything would calm down. Also, it was perfect because I was on holiday in August and I fancied getting to know the country. It couldn't have been better.

"Of course I'm in!"

"I can take you to Real de Catorce," Antonio offered. "I have to go there this Saturday…"

"We accept," my friend replied straight away. "We'll travel together to try the peyote."

"I'll take you, but you must be careful with the peyote; as you've already seen many people lose their minds…"

"Pass me another beer and let's toast," my friend ordered, laughing.

"To the *pinche* trip!" the three of us toasted, cheerfully.

And that was how it was finally decided.

Without that trip, everything would have been different and my friend would still be alive.

Damn trip.

Everything went wrong from the very beginning.

Antonio told us that the trip had to be delayed due to a clandestine cockfight. His pal's cocks were taking part and he couldn't miss it, and he invited us to go with him. The plan was for us to go together to the fight and then set off for Real de Catorce straight away. My friend was excited.

We approached the backyard of the house where the fights were going to take place. Everything was ready when we arrived. Although it was a pretty shabby place, a morbidly obese guy charged us a few pesos to let us in.

"Do you charge to enter here?" I asked, surprised.

"No, *güey*. It's a fund for *mordidas* [bribes], to pay the police so they don't come here. It's to make sure that they're busy with other matters this morning. There're a lot of crimes in this city, as you know," Antonio said, winking at me.

As soon as we went in, everybody there turned to look at us. We were the last ones to arrive and we drew attention to ourselves. Surrounded by those people wearing cowboy hats and typical Mexican boots, all of them with huge moustaches, my friend and I looked like doctors in a mine. Those present didn't look exactly like dog groomers or interior decorators. They were ruffians, thieves, bandits and narcs, the best of every house, the elite of the underworld. Unsurprisingly, Antonio's buddy, the owner of some of the cocks that were fighting, had been in jail. He went by the peculiar name of Little Al, although he wasn't little and I doubt he was called Al either. His arms were covered in faded tattoos and he had a pock-marked face. When we shook hands, mine got lost in his like a fish inside a lake. The pressure was so brutal that I felt my bones crack and hardly managed to disguise my pain. In the meantime, a circle was cleared out for the fights in the centre of the backyard.

They put very sharp blades on the cocks' spurs to ensure the fight is to the death. It only lasts a few seconds. The coaches bring them closer so they face each other, then move back, leaving one metre of distance between the animals, and set them free. The roosters lunge at each other and you can only see a crash, wings beating and feathers flying. Afterwards, at least one of them drops to the floor. When they pick it up, it has a huge cut from which cascades of blood flow. If the animal isn't dead, the coach sucks from its beak the remains of blood and mucus accumulated so it can breathe. He spits on the floor that disgusting mixture and, if the cock is able to, they start again. Often the winner is so torn to bits that it ends up dying too.

People would bet in each fight. We, advised by Antonio, started betting and losing money. When there were only the last few cocks left to fight, Antonio and Little Al moved slightly away from the group to talk.

Antonio came and told us to bet all of our money on the rival cock. I looked at my friend, who nodded. What happened next was so fast that I remember it like flashes in my memory: we bet, the roosters got entangled, ours fell with a huge cut to the throat, Little Al checked that it was dead and quickly removed its blades, I collected all the money we had won, people began to mumble, insults and pushing started, Antonio and his buddy got us out of the circle that was forming around us, we left the premises, turned the corner, started to run, reached Antonio's old car, jumped in, a guy put an enormous suitcase in the boot and Antonio ordered me to give him all the money we'd won. I hesitated a beat and he shouted at me.

"Give it to him already! *Ahorita*!"

I gave him the money through the window and we set off so quickly that the tyres screeched on the asphalt.

Before I had a chance to digest what had happened, our car was already skidding through the narrow streets of that neighbourhood. The sudden turns made us slide from side to side, shaking us up as if we were dolls. Antonio was totally focused on his driving, and the rest of us kept quiet. The atmosphere was very tense inside that car and I was stunned, disconcerted. We reached larger streets, with more traffic, and we slowed down to an almost normal speed. My perplexity began to fade and it was replaced by terror. 'My God!' I thought, horrified. 'What have we done?' On understanding the magnitude of the mess Antonio had got us into, fear was slowly replaced by fury.

"What the fuck is this? What mess did you get us into, son of a bitch?"

He didn't reply. From the backseat, I peered into the rear-view mirror to see his face. I noticed that he quickly looked away. That emboldened me and I began to shout at him, banging on his seat at the same time.

"Can't you even look at me, you son of a bitch? What were you thinking about when you took us there? Fucking bastard!"

Little Al turned around, looked me straight in the eye and said, very slowly:

"Be quiet and close your *pinche* mouth or I'll kill you."

I went quiet. The furious look of that delinquent scared the shit out of me. That guy seemed capable of anything. I looked at my friend, who was smiling and seemed calm. He gave me a nod to let it go, a typical gesture of his that people use when it's a matter of no importance. While doing that, he started to talk.

"I'm going to tell you a story that's extremely appropriate to these circumstances. It shows, exactly, what I'm trying to tell you."

We all waited expectantly.

"I met a guy in Austin, Texas, who was the champion of throwing olive stones. That guy had a gift: he could spit an olive's stone up to an impressive distance. So good was he that he managed to win the world championship five years in a row, something really unheard of in those types of competitions. We Spaniards have a great tradition of throwing olives, not surprising as we have the best olive trees in the world; Italians have a long tradition of olive trees and olives, and, of course, the Greeks have been cultivating olives for centuries. Well, that fucking guy from Austin, Texas, was able to put to shame the best specialists of all those Mediterranean countries for a whole lustrum. He beat people who are born with an olive under their pillows, so to speak. His trick, apart from his lung capacity, was the large size of his tongue. He was capable of folding it, as if it were a bellows, and then propelling the olive pit to a distance unreachable for the rest of mortals. In fact, his nickname was Snake Tongue. When he obtained his fifth and last title, he decided to buy a snake with the money he'd won. Nobody but him knows the reason why. Perhaps he wanted a pretty and nice reminder that would keep him company, perhaps he wanted to highlight and idealise his nickname. Whatever the reason, he bought one of these huge anacondas, a critter of a massive size. Well, one day the snake escaped from the gigantic terrariums where he kept it, reached the street and ate a toddler that was playing in the garden of his house. They had to sacrifice the snake and open it in half to get the dead child out. Do you know what the moral of this fucking story is? What am I trying to tell you? What should we learn from this? That in this life sometimes it's our turn to be the anaconda and others we have to be the child, but you should never visit *pinche* Texas if you don't have a very good reason to."

I looked at him incredulously. Antonio and Little Al looked at each other for a second and burst out laughing.

"No, seriously, that guy later sold it to an exotic food restaurant. They say those animals are an aphrodisiac. People are not well, not at all."

They couldn't stop laughing. It was a childish and nervous laughter, unstoppable after the accumulated tension. Tears were running down their cheeks, they were flushed and neither one of them could stop. On the contrary, the laughter of one got the other one going, in an endless vicious circle. In the end, they managed to get even me to smile.

When the laughs ended, the tension had dissipated. They all seem to be in a good mood, except for me. We had cheated some delinquents, some unsavoury characters. Those people wouldn't give up just like that; they didn't look like that kind of people. They'd look for us, they'd catch us and they'd kill us. I remembered Antonio had mentioned I was living at the International House. It wouldn't be difficult for them to find me; I had all my things there and I had to go back for them. They had all my information and that of my family in Spain there. Blessed be God! What would happen? I was terrified.

My friend, looking like a jolly rogue, interrupted my thoughts.

"Will you tell me the trick? What did we do to lose the fight? It was something to do with the blades, wasn't it?"

Antonio and his buddy exchanged a knowing look and smiled. Antonio spoke.

"It's easy. If you tie the blade farther up than usual, the hits with the spur lose power and precision. It's very silly because it's so simple. The only issue is that one has to do it well to avoid being caught. This time my buddy wasn't sharp enough."

The other started to get angry.

"Don't be a dumbass! My cock was so good that if I didn't put them very high up, it would have won anyway. Nobody noticed, man. The Spaniard couldn't see it."

"I didn't see it, really," my friend intervened. "I only noticed that you removed the blades very quickly and that made me suspicious that something was afoot. Nothing else."

I was following the conversation attentively but wasn't taking part. I was too anxious and sad. What did the issue of the blades matter now? I only asked Antonio the question that was making me angriest.

"Did you get us into all this mess on purpose? I thought you were my friend…"

"No, man, not at all! I thought we'd win the money much easier, but everything started going wrong and we needed that money. It's the truth. Otherwise, we would have been in even worse trouble. In this life, one has to improvise, my man, grab it as it comes. If you lose your nerve they bury you, that's all. Don't get sad, it all went well. Don't scream like an old woman."

"You're telling me not to scream? Those people know where I live and how to find me. They could even find the information about my family in Spain! Are you telling me to improvise and not shout? After the mess you've got us into?"

"Don't you worry so. They also know where I work and where my family lives. We'll bribe them with a bit of money. When we come to the end of this trip we'll have plenty..."

"Or with some lead," his buddy added cheerfully.

They both laughed.

"We're going to get lots of money; I'll give back all the money I owe. Don't spoil it, man; life smiles at us, we're alive and we'll be rich. What else could we ask for?"

I shook my head and let it drop. It was useless to keep talking to those brainless idiots. There's nothing to worry about. What a fucking joke! We had cheated on a group of delinquents and were carrying something suspicious inside the boot of the car.

The journey seemed to last forever. My friend was sleeping like a baby and Antonio was talking and joking with Little Al. I was sitting in the back, frightened, trying to cheer myself up. I was trying to convince myself that there would be no problems, but I didn't manage it.

It was almost night-time when we arrived. The stars were starting to fill up the sky and the freezing darkness was slowly enveloping us with no nearby light offering any resistance. Antonio seemed to know the road well; he drove at a good speed through that track that was becoming faint. He left the main route via a T-junction and drove on until it stopped in front of a lonely shack on top of a headland. One could discern Real de Catorce at a distance. Those four dirty and flaky walls gave the place a ghostly look. Its evident state of neglect suggested it had been uninhabited for quite a while.

Antonio furtively flashed the lights of his old car, twice. From inside of the house, they replied in kind. Once he had received the sign, he switched off the engine. The engine's fan still purred for a bit before stopping and leaving us surrounded by a silence that flooded everything. Little Al got out of the car. His footsteps sounded clumsy and slow on the gravel of the ground; his legs were still half asleep from the long trip. He went to the back of the car. Once there, we could clearly hear the sound of the lighter and the couple of deep drags he gave the cigarette before he opened the boot. With the suitcase in one hand and the cigarette in the other, he set off towards the house, walking in a way that looked deliberately slow. When he reached the door, he waited without knocking.

Suddenly there was a sharp noise, which I learned later was the sound a weapon shot with a silencer makes. For a short instant, nothing happened and Antonio's buddy stayed standing a few seconds before he collapsed. Then he dropped dead like a puppet whose strings have been cut.

Chapter 7. Problems

We were alone in that lost beach at the bottom of the cliff and I could no longer see my friend. He'd jumped into the sea to find out what was inside the ghost yacht and had disappeared. Now he was a ghost too. I pulled on the rope he had tied around his waist and saw it was as tense as before. At least he hadn't disappeared completely; ghosts don't weigh anything.

After a while, I saw him resurface and felt an enormous relief. He was waving, trying to tell me something, but I couldn't understand him. It looked as if he was manipulating the rope. Suddenly I noticed it was slackening. He had untied it! He looked at me, took a deep breath and dove in next to the mast. I felt very scared and started to gather up the rope. I did it mechanically, without paying attention, while my gaze remained trained on the mast of the sunken yacht, to the spot where he'd gone diving. After some time, when I had collected it all, he came to the surface of the water. It took me a while to locate him because he reappeared quite far away from where he'd swum under. Then I shouted, gesticulating to make him come back to the shore, but he didn't hear me, or didn't understand me, or didn't want to do as I asked. To my desperation, instead of coming out, he repeated the same operation several times more. It was agonising: every time I thought it had been the last time, he'd go under again. Although it's true that his immersions were getting shorter and the time he spent catching his breath after each attempt grew longer. Finally, I saw he'd decided to put an end to it. He waved at me and started swimming towards me. At first, he tried to do it stylishly but he didn't manage to advance; then he tried it with less style but more energy. It didn't work either. He was trying to swim towards the shore and he couldn't manage it; the current was too strong and he didn't have the same strength as he had at the beginning.

Impotent, I looked towards the long rope that was coiled in big circles over my arm, and then I looked back at my reckless friend. The effort he'd made during the immersions had notably weakened him. The current was very strong and he wasn't capable of overcoming it. He was trying to counteract its effect by swimming as hard as he could, but the only thing he achieved was to stay in place, without being dragged backwards.

"Damn!" I shouted.

I tied the rope to my waist quickly, I checked that it remained firmly tied to the rock and jumped into the water. I had to rescue him before the current pulled him away.

To swim with a rope tied around your waist isn't easy at all. When the current tightens it, it pulls you back a lot. I wasn't a great swimmer, but I wasn't doing too badly. I was rested and I was swimming with extraordinary energy; the fear of losing my friend gave me strength. Also, I had started swimming a bit farther on from where he was, and therefore the current helped me a bit. I progressed slowly, with great effort until finally, after much paddling, I reached him.

"Hold on to my feet!" I shouted, exhausted, while I held on to the rope with my hands and I floated on my back.

In such a funny fashion we managed to get close to the shore, but it wasn't easy. I couldn't move my legs; he was holding on to them; I couldn't move my arms to swim either because they were busy pulling the rope. I swallowed lots of water.

When we finally reached the shore, we were light-headed due to the effort. We crawled to the sand and there we lay, exhausted. We were breathing so hard that our ribs and stomachs were like an accordion at a concert. Our hearts seemed about to burst out of our chests.

Several minutes passed before we were able to get up. The first thing I did was to remove the rope I was wearing, which had left a deep abrasion on me. I looked at my friend who had the same wound.

"The mark of the pirates," he boasted, smiling.

"You're an asshole! We nearly drowned," I protested, irate. "Don't start your nonsense."

"You've saved me; if it wasn't for you, I'd be in Ireland by now."

"What the fuck do you think we tied you for?"

"You're really foul-mouthed, goodness me! I'm going to have to wash your mouth with soap," he scolded me, mockingly.

"Ass-ho-le! Do you understand me? You're an asshole. We nearly drowned because of your stupidity. It's time you stopped playing stupid," I shouted, annoyed.

"I had to untie it; it didn't allow me to dive to the bottom. I couldn't see what was inside of the boat."

"In that case, you should have turned around and we would have looked for another way to do it. Nobody would have thought of letting the rope go!"

"There was no other way."

I was mad and I didn't want to argue with him. I knew it was a waste of time; either he laughed at you or he cleverly got you on his side. I stayed quiet, turned around and looked the other way, turning my back on him. A damn friend and a damn ghost yacht.

He left me alone for a couple of minutes, and then he stood up and planted himself squarely in front of me. He started walking in an absolutely ridiculous way, pushing his ass back and bending his legs. I turned to avoid seeing him, but he repeated the operation until he appeared again in my field of vision and started walking again in such a peculiar way.

"The dance of the camel without twisting the neck!" he shouted, repeatedly, while he carried on with his funny walk.

I tried to control my laughter and keep serious. I didn't want to forgive him so quickly, but I must have let something show because he grew in confidence.

"Shall I tell you what I've seen there? It's incredible!"

I couldn't resist any longer.

"Weeell… What have you seeeen?" I conceded, with a slight smile.

"Let's start climbing back up; it's getting late and it isn't a good idea to stay here when it gets dark. I'll tell you on the way."

How typical of my friend. He always did the same once he managed to get my attention. He loved to play hard to get! Then, when he finally started telling you the story, instead of offering you a short head-line, a summary, he liked to tell everything slowly, enjoying the little details, even going off on a tangent that had nothing to do with it. Anything to keep the expectation until the end.

We started going up calmly and, finally, he started talking.

"I've seen the sunken yacht. It was at the bottom, stuck between several huge rocks, that's why it remains in a vertical position. I dove down to see if I could get in. The problem is that the current was very strong and I had to work hard to fight against it. I tried to hold on to the mast and push myself, but that made me go slower. After several attempts, I finally managed to reach the rocks at the bottom where the yacht was. The hatchway was open (it's odd that they left it open, perhaps that was why it sunk). Well, the thing is that I didn't go in; I worried I might get stuck on something and not be able to get out. However, the important thing wasn't what was inside of the yacht, but what was outside."

"Get to the point!" I pleaded, impatient.

"Don't interrupt me. Do you want me to tell you what I saw? I saw ropes coming out of the yacht. At the other end, they had bags tied up with plumb lines acting as ballast..."

"What were they?" I interrupted, surprised.

"They were plasticised parcels, full of drugs."

"Great. Are you telling me you nearly drowned for a few drug parcels? Now I feel reassured. Now everything makes sense," I exclaimed, ironically.

"Don't get upset, man," he said and started climbing again.

We carried on going up the steep cliff and, once we got to the top, we couldn't see the bag that marked the entry to the path between the furzes. I got quite worked up.

"Where is the bag? Are you sure that you tied it up well? Will it have flown away?"

"I tied it up well," he asserted, puzzled. "Don't worry; if we check carefully I'm sure we'll find the path anyway."

We started looking, but we didn't manage to find the entry. The furzes created a wide insurmountable wall. Everything looked the same and we couldn't find any points of reference to guide us. It was getting dark and I got anxious.

"It's getting dark. We'll have to spend the night here. Do your parents know, at least, that we were coming here?"

"Haven't you told your parents either?" he asked, amused.

"Now we're truly fucked," I replied, getting increasingly anxious.

"Stop moaning about it and let's keep looking," he ordered, smiling. "Don't you want to spend the night with me in such a romantic place, darling?"

"It's not funny. I've had enough of your crap. They'll kill me at home…"

"If the cliff doesn't kill you first," he noted, mockingly.

"I've told you to stop joking about it! It's enough!"

"OK, don't get stressed. Up to now, we've been stumbling about both of us together; now we'll separate and we'll divide the task. We'll go inch by inch, calmly and systematically."

We had to rush; there was hardly any light left. I tried to calm down and be thorough, but I couldn't see the entry. I was starting to feel desperate when, suddenly, I heard him shout.

"I found it! It's here!"

I felt truly liberated. We were saved! I ran to the place he was pointing out; we had no time to lose. We came out of the maze of furzes and crossed the forest of eucalyptus. He was a couple of steps ahead of me. We were about to reach the house of Dark Shadow when the horrible man stepped out from behind a tree and hit my friend with a eucalyptus branch. It was a hard blow right in the stomach. My poor friend fell to the floor, breathless. I couldn't move, terrified, frozen. Dark Shadow was blocking my way, holding the branch up high.

Chapter 8. Real de Catorce

They had shot Little Al and we were immobilised by fear and surprise. Antonio could not react.

"Drive on!" shouted my friend.

Antonio was so frightened that when he tried to start the car he stalled it. Two guys came out of the house pointing at him with their guns.

"Don't you dare move, *güey*, or you'll join your friend right this moment."

They walked towards us always with their guns trained on him. One of them planted himself in front of Antonio's window, which was open, and ordered him to get out of the car.

"Put your hands on your head and kneel down."

Antonio, who was quite fat, had difficulty getting into that position; he moved slowly and clumsily. In the meantime, the other gunman placed himself in front of my door, pointing his gun at me. He came one step closer and knocked softly on the window with the gun's silencer, gesturing for me to lower it down. I froze. Then he knocked again, this time louder, and pointed straight between my eyebrows. My friend moved me to one side and lowered the glass pane.

"Come out and kneel down!"

The night's icy wind sent a shiver all over my body. Freezing and horrified, I was petrified and couldn't move at all.

"I don't want to kill you. The police will have to get working if a couple of foreign students go missing. And, you'll have to run an errand for me to make me spare your *pinches* lives. However, it's a different matter with the fatty; we can kill him."

"We'll do whatever you want," my friend interjected, quickly, "but we'll need a chauffeur. Neither of us can drive."

"Don't fuck with me! Don't tell me you can't drive?"

We both shook our heads.

"Don't shoot the fatty. *Pinches* Spaniards! Good for nothing!"

"He isn't fat, it's water retention," my friend replied, very serious.

Both gunmen barked a brief guffaw.

"Well, let's stop this nonsense and get in."

After patting us down and taking away our passports, they guided us to the house. We walked past Little Al. He was dead, lying in front of the door. I tried to avert my eyes and I couldn't; he had a big bloodstain around his head. When we had passed him we heard another sharp impact and we turned around, startled. The man behind us had shot the body again.

"Just in case," he said, very serious. "I don't turn my back on anybody, not even my mum."

"Better that way," replied the other one while he picked up the suitcase that had fallen next to the lifeless body.

We entered a big and empty room. The only thing there was a sofa, dilapidated and dirty, by one of the walls. They waved at us to sit on it. Squeezed against each other and with the broken springs sticking into our backs, we waited with our heads lowered. They stood there, with their guns in their hands. The one who'd entered last, and who seemed to be the boss, started to talk.

"We're businessmen. Our businesses are based on the capitalist economy of the free market. We have something to offer you and you have something to offer us. It's the law of supply and demand. We are offering you something immensely valuable: we offer you your lives. Nothing is worth more; life is a recipient that can be filled with anything. From you, we demand a very powerful instrument: money. Therefore, you also offer us something very valuable: you offer us opportunities. You might think money is something mundane and dirty compared to life, but there are lives that are mundane and dirty too. I've offered you an empty bowl; you can fill it with anything; I won't judge you. You're giving me a powerful instrument that I can use to achieve any goal; don't judge me. We can talk about life and this will be a life negotiation. We can talk about death and this will be a death negotiation. I've come to offer life to you. What do you say?"

I stared at him, numb.

"We want life," replied my friend.

"Very well. We understand each other. Now I'll
show you my hand. Excuse me for talking so slowly,
as if I were talking to people of limited understanding, of little intelligence. It's my way of addressing
idiots. After the little number of the cockfight, you
don't deserve anything else. Did you think that
information wouldn't reach me? That I wouldn't
make use of it? Taking into account what happened, it
seems you didn't think about it, therefore I treat you
according to the IQ you've shown. Well, I carry on; I
don't want you to lose the thread. The cards I hold
are the following: I have the addresses of your
accommodations and that of your families because I
have the passports of the Spaniards and the address
of the fatty; therefore, I'll entrust you with an easy
job. You must go to the North, to the city of Monclova, in the state of Coahuila. Once you're in Monclova,
you'll go to the church of Santiago Apóstol (a very
cool church, as it happens). There you must contact
Pancho, the Tarahumara. I won't tell you what you
have to do afterwards to avoid overtaxing your little
brains. Just concentrate on driving there. Today is
Sunday and you must turn up there next Sunday.
You have exactly one week, more than enough time. I
won't go with you; I like to trust people. If you get
lost, if you try to be too clever, I'll find you, even if I
have to go to Spain to look for you. I'll kill you; I'll
kill your daddies, your mommies, your siblings… I'll
even kill your *pinches* dogs. Remember, memorise:
Monclova, church of Santiago Apóstol, Pancho, the
Tarahumara. Once you get in touch with the Tarahumara you'll have fulfilled your deal with me. That
and the bag of drugs you've brought me and are

giving me as a gift, of course. Once you've finished the job that Pancho will entrust you, you'll have fulfilled your obligation towards the people you've stolen from at the cockfight. Is it all clear? Any questions?"

We didn't reply.

"Everything clear?! Any *pinche* questions?"

"Everything clear," my friend replied. "Monclova, church of Santiago Apóstol, Pancho, the Tarahumara."

"I underestimated you. You're *pinches* geniuses memorising stuff. My goodness, what retentive capacity, *güey*. I bow to you," he mocked while he copied the passport addresses.

He returned them to us and added:

"If anybody asks you, it's very easy: you've never been in this house and you've never seen us. Is that clear?"

We nodded.

"Go fuck yourselves! I don't want to see you ever again, dumbasses."

We stood up clumsily and left that house. We got into the car with a heavy heart. Antonio started the car, this time without any problems.

I looked through the car window as we pulled away. Behind us, we left the sinister house with the two figures by the door and the body at their feet. That is the image that has stuck with me.

As I looked at Little Al, I thought of how close life and death are, how one can go from one to the other without any fuss, without any transitional periods.

Life slips from our hands and it never comes back. It's something as valuable as it is easy to lose. Perhaps that fragility is what gives it its worth.

When we left that house I was demoralised and sad. Little by little, the sadness turned into fear and that into terror. Antonio had also lost his usual nonchalance towards life; I saw him downcast and nervous. We were in a terrible mess. My friend had remained quite quiet and, compared to his usual behaviour, he hadn't been very active. Even with that, he'd still prevented them from killing Antonio and had reacted quickly when I was frozen and couldn't open the window. The worst thing was that, as far as I could remember, he was capable of much more. That worried me. I thought perhaps he had changed during those years, although I also considered, and this worried me more, that the situation was so serious that even he was in over his head. Perhaps I had idolised him. After all, he wasn't a superhero. The only thing I was clear about was that if my friend lost his cool, we would be truly fucked.

Then he interrupted my thoughts.

"Stop thinking about dead lizards."

"What?"

"You're both there, quiet, looking panicked, thinking of dead lizards. That's not helping us an iota."

"Go fuck your mother, you bastard. My buddy is dead. What do you want me to think about?"

"Yes. Your buddy is dead. That's a done deed that you shouldn't worry about because it has no remedy.

You're alive and that's important. You mustn't lose your cool. When I was a child and I got panicky, they taught me to think of dead lizards. I imagined myself walking through a huge marble palace with big rooms. The cold floor of the palace was covered in dead lizards, piled up in such a way that they formed a thick layer. I walked over them and I could feel my feet sinking into their bodies. As I walked over their bodies, softened by decomposition, their ribs cracked with my footsteps. I heard a kind of noise: chop-chop-crunch-chop. Then I thought that there were no more dead lizards and everything was sorted. I no longer had as many problems and my anxiety reduced."

I looked at him, angrily. I wasn't sure which option I liked the least: the thought that such a story could be true or, that it was all a lie and he had dared to tell such a macabre joke. Whatever the case was, he was mad; he was sick.

Antonio shook his head. He was quiet for a few seconds and then muttered:

"Dead lizards, eh? OK, *güey*, it's done. What do you want me to think about now?"

"Let's go looking for Doña Toña in San Antonio de Coronados and let's try the peyote."

"Are you an idiot?" I shouted, unable to restrain myself. "We only have a week to go looking for Pancho, the Tarahumara."

"You've said it: we have a week. It's too long. We only need, at a push, a couple of days. If we get there too early we might get into further problems. We have to pass the time, and the best thing to do is to find some distraction. And, I have some questions to ask Mezcalito."

Incredibly enough, Antonio took his side. Nothing better than to go and visit somebody we knew in the area and not connected at all to our business. I was on my own. I couldn't do anything, so I decided neither to argue nor to talk to them anymore. Simply, I'd let things go and I'd take advantage of the silence and meditate. I needed time to clarify my ideas and to elaborate a good plan, but, what plan? We couldn't escape, we couldn't ask for anybody's help and we didn't know what we were going to face. We had no other option but to wait. What a plan.

Chapter 9. Whining

Dark Shadow had just hit my friend with a eucalyptus branch and was blocking me with the raised stick. He screamed, in Galician:

"You aren't going to steal from my traps ever again. Fucking sons of bitches!"

It took me a few seconds to react. Once I did, I scrutinised the scene, instinctively, trying to find a way out avoiding the path Dark Shadow was blocking. He read my thoughts. He got hold of my friend and pulled him up, grabbing him by his T-shirt. The poor boy didn't resist; he hadn't caught his breath back yet.

"Are you going to leave him here alone?"

"Are you mad? We haven't done anything! I'll go to the police."

"You didn't do anything, you say? Didn't you steal from my traps?"

"They were illegal!"

Betrayed by nerves and fear, I made a mistake. My friend always said that when they accuse you of something you must go for the big denial. Deny everything: don't only say that you didn't do it, you weren't even there. That thought flashed through my mind. I thought, angrily, that it was too late.

"Did you steal from my traps because they were illegal? Very well, you're right, they were illegal! The only problem is that, as I can't report you, we'll have to solve it in some other way... Because I swear that you'll pay for it."

Then he hit my friend again with the eucalyptus branch. Taking advantage of the distraction, I approached him and got hold of the stick, trying to get it off him, but he was much stronger than me. He pulled from the branch we both were holding and I was propelled towards him. When he had me close enough, he gave me such a slap that he threw me on the floor. I experienced a huge pain. The explosion of the slap on my ear left me dizzy. The hands of that man were like an ogre's: enormous and hard. It was as if I'd been hit by a wooden plank.

Now, we were both on the floor, literally at his feet. Dark Shadow was still holding up the stick, threatening, prepared to bring it down on whoever moved. My eyes were damp, tears on the verge of flowing. Impotence and pain had made my resistance collapse. The only thing that prevented me from crying was feeling ashamed that he'd witness it, but I knew I wouldn't be able to hold on for much longer. I wanted to talk and I realised that if I did, I'd cry. I wouldn't be able to hold back the tears if I opened my mouth. On the verge of crying, I looked at the floor so it wouldn't show and didn't move. To my surprise, my friend went to pieces. He started whining.

"Don't beat us up anymore, please, don't hit us anymore," he whined. "It hurts a lot! We'll pay you."

Dark Shadow stayed put, pleased with himself. I didn't feel like crying any longer and stared at my friend, astonished. Now I was proud of myself. I'd been harder than him. This time I had taught him a lesson.

"Don't hit us anymore, please," my friend insisted. "I know a way to compensate you."

"How, fucker, how?" asked Dark Shadow, unable to hide his greed.

And then, my friend told him about the drug parcels in the sunken yacht.

I was listening to him and couldn't believe it. Still whining, he told him everything we had seen that day. He was mad! When he finished talking, Dark Shadow thought for a moment, and then started threatening us.

"This is what we'll do: you won't say anything to anybody about this. If you talk to anyone, I promise you I'll kill you. I'll wait until you're alone: one afternoon at a small beach or one evening as you go home… I'll wait for the best moment, I swear."

"No. We won't say anything," whined my friend. "I swear. We won't say anything. We don't want any problems. We're scared by all this. The police could arrest us… If they discover it, they'll send us to jail. It would be terrible!"

Again, I kept quiet. His attitude appeared undignified to me. A single hit and he'd crumbled and chickened out. Dark Shadow stared at me.

"And what do you think?"

"The same as me. He won't say anything," he reassured him, crying.

"I want to hear that from the mouth of your brave friend. I wouldn't want us to have a misunderstanding of any kind."

I didn't want to repeat the cowardly and yielding words of my friend. With a dignified attitude, whereby I tried to portray weariness rather than fear, I only said:

"I don't want to know anything else about this. I won't say anything."

He seemed to weigh my reply for a few seconds. Finally, he was satisfied.

"Good. Get out of here!"

We stood up, clumsily, and moved away. In silence, we got to the place where we'd left our bikes. The bastard had burst our tyres. I noticed anger in my friend's eyes; he'd shown me how to detect those kinds of things. 'Too late now!' I thought. After having behaved that way…

We had to go back home walking, dragging the bikes with us. When we were a certain distance from there, he was the one who broke the silence.

"How did I do?" he asked, laughing.

"What do you mean?"

"I'm asking how I did."

"What have you done?"

"Pretended to be scared. Whine…"

"Don't tell me now that…"

He burst out laughing and he imitated his previous whining: "Please, don't beat us anymore. Boo-hoo. Boo-hoo."

I looked at him, closely. I was unable to tell when he was lying and when he wasn't.

"'It would be terrible.' Didn't you find it funny when I used that phrase?"

"Fuck!" I conceded. "So, everything was humbug? You've made yourself look like a whiner and a coward for nothing? What's the point of that? I don't believe you."

"There is a very good point. I have a plan."

"Don't bother telling me! I believe you and that's it. Now I believe you, don't tell me anything else, please. I don't want to get into any more messes; I don't want any problems."

"In this life, there are always problems. You can run away, but they'll be waiting for you when you come back. If you hide, they'll find you. The only way to solve them is to face them fearlessly, decisively. Only when you accept that you'll have to face them all your life, fighting day in and day out without a break, you'll manage to live in peace. When you run away, people quickly sense your weakness and many more problems crop up. For each confrontation you avoid, three new ones appear."

"Don't quote phrases from mafia movies…"

"They aren't from mafia movies. They are from my father."

I was left speechless. I wanted to say something, but I dismissed it. I didn't want to offend his father. Better to keep my peace.

"You've done well," he pointed out.

I felt flattered.

"I've left you alone and you've borne it bravely. Neither tears nor concessions."

"And I also defended you," I added. "I've ended up receiving a good slap for trying to remove his stick."

"That's also true. Remind me to show you one day a trick to disarm somebody carrying a stick."

"I can see it worked very well for you," I replied, stung.

"You're as fast as usual," he affirmed, smiling. "The blow took me by surprise and I couldn't use any tricks. Don't get upset, man, I was only trying to help you…"

Night fell. A pitch-black sky, covered in stars, accompanied us to the village. It was late. Getting home at such a time would earn me a telling-off for sure. After everything that had happened, I was in a foul mood.

"Seriously, don't you want me to tell you my plan? It's genius. It will be very funny."

"No, I don't want you to; I don't feel like it," I cut him off, curtly.

"OK, OK…"

We got to the village and we went each our own way. I got home and my parents reprimanded me. It was to be expected.

"Where have you been?"

"Around, on the bike. We climbed up the track and we had two flat tyres. It got late while we tried to repair them. We had to come back walking and dragging the bikes, and that made us even later."

"You're going to bed without supper. You're grounded the whole day tomorrow."

"Perfect," I retorted, cockily.

"Double punishment: you're grounded tomorrow and the day after. We were thinking about allowing you to go out as it was the last day of our holiday, but you asked for it. Any other comments?"

I thought about adding something else, but I desisted; it was a lost battle. I turned around and went to my room. Lying on my bed, I couldn't sleep; I was chewing my revenge over non-stop. I was so mad that my bad mood had made my tiredness disappear. My pride hurt with Dark Shadow's slap, and on top of that, the bikes! It got to the early hours of the morning and I was still recreating in my head the images of the beating I'd give that fucking bastard someday. When I grew older, I would crack his head in two. He would have to bear a shower of kicks and punches; I would beat him to a pulp...

The fabulous thing was that I didn't need to do any of that. Next summer I discovered that his very expensive bull turned up dead a few days after I left. He was lying on his side, swollen like a balloon. When his marvellous bull died, Dark Shadow went mad with anger. A day later, his house burned to ashes. The bells of the church rang, warning the population about the fire, but nobody got there in time. It was very far away from the village and the people who turned up did it slowly. I was happy when I heard the news; bad people deserve bad things happening to them.

After those misfortunes, Dark Shadow disappeared from the village. Several summers went by and I forgot all about it until it resurfaced again...

Chapter 10. Doña Toña and the Dragon

Finding the village of San Antonio de Coronados wasn't complicated. After following the track that coasted from hilly Real de Catorce, we found the place easily. It consisted only of a few houses spread around a simple church. They were modest adobe buildings, matching the surrounding desert. The floating dust gave a uniform shade to the picture: the houses, the few cars there, the terrain and even the inhabitants, everything was covered in that sandy tapestry that penetrated up to the tiniest corner. When we asked for Doña Toña, a skinny and dried-up individual gave us accurate directions to her house, only using a few words. It was a simple building, in keeping with the rest of the village, that only differed from the others because it had a little garden at the back.

We knocked at the door and Doña Toña in person opened it. She was a lovely old lady. Short and plump, wearing a blue apron, her image was that of a devoted and kind person. Her hair, whiter than white and held up in a bun, gave her face a gentle appearance. The deep crow's feet suggested she was a very cheerful person.

Showing us great hospitality, she invited us to go in before we were able to say anything. Inside, the house was totally austere, the only poetic indulgence was a bucket of flowers placed in the middle of a small table. The cleanness was absolutely exquisite, not a single speck of the perennial dust was allowed in that place. It must have been very hard to manage…

After having a sip of the coffee she'd offered us, my friend got talking.

"We come on behalf of Peter Marco. He told us we should get in touch with you."

"Mmm… Yes. Peter Marco. Yes. A young man with problems, but very pleasant. How are things with him?" she asked in a kind and affectionate tone.

"Well, we can't tell you much. We met him one evening, having a few beers in a canteen. He asked us to greet you on his behalf."

"You come looking for peyote, no?" the good woman guessed, insightfully.

"Yes," replied my friend, honestly. "Peter Marco recommended you very highly and did the same with the peyote. Do you recommend us to try it?"

"What each individual does is his or her own business," she replied, kindly but firmly. "That's something you need to decide for yourselves. If you want to, I can introduce you to my nephew. He knows how to find it in the desert. He won't charge you much."

"We'd like to meet him."

Doña Toña offered us somewhere to stay and lent us blankets, water decanters and a tarpaulin to sleep on at the back. The garden was wide and simple; it had a central area with plants and sufficient space around it for us to lie down without being crowded. Knowing we had the accommodation ensured, we asked the granny to guide us in search of her nephew. She said goodbye, after introducing him to us, and asked us to enter directly via the garden if we got there late.

The nephew was repairing the window of his house. He was a dark-haired guy, short and lean. He was wearing disgusting jeans and an old and torn T-shirt. As was to be expected, he was covered in the omnipresent fine dust. The expression on his face was a bit simple-minded and he opened his eyes very wide when he talked.

"If you want peyote, you'll have to pay me."

"Will this be enough?" my friend asked, offering him a generous amount of cash.

"Of course," he replied, opening his eyes even more.

"Can we go right now?"

"Of course. Mmm… Are you coming with me?"

"Of course," my friend replied with a serious expression that hid a subtle hint of mockery.

Antonio preferred to wait for us at the village; he didn't want anything to do with the peyote. I hesitated. I was tired, but I thought that a short walk would help me clear my mind. The night was falling; it couldn't be that far…

"Let's go."

He dropped the hammer with which he was repairing the window and left at full speed. We looked at each other in amazement at his sudden reaction and ran quickly to catch up with him. We crossed the dusty and empty streets of the village in a flash, without meeting anybody. The desert started there. Many groups of small bushes, like the creosote bush, peppered the barren terrain we were walking on. Some cacti and agavaceae broke a bit the monotony of the landscape. There were many grooves and we had to jump or go up and down, according to their size. Advancing was complicated and the speed that guy was imposing was devilish. My friend was able to keep up with him, but I started to fall back. I was exhausted and had difficulty breathing. The area where we were was over two thousand metres in height and the lack of oxygen was noticeable. It was getting dark, but the heat was still suffocating in the desert. I was sweating buckets, was thirsty and had no water. I never thought we'd be going so far.

When I was about to give up, the guide reduced his pace. Then he started to move from bush to bush. He looked carefully, then took out his penknife and dug in the soil. When I managed to get close to him, I saw them: at ground level, there were strange circular shaped objects of sizes varying from a big coin to a small medal. They were dark green, but they were not easily visible until he pointed them out. He dug the knife into the soil and cut them from underneath to get them out. Then he extracted a kind of pill with wedges. According to him, the females had more wedges – eight or ten – and the males fewer – around five. He picked up many and put them inside a dirty handkerchief he carried.

The desert turned orange with the final sun rays. Doña Toña's nephew looked thoughtfully at the horizon and told us we had to go back. We went back at the same speed at which we'd got there as if we were fleeing something or somebody. When we caught sight of the village from afar I relaxed and I followed them at a distance that kept increasing. When I finally got there, my friend had already said goodbye to the guy.

"Let's go to Doña Toña's house."

I wasn't able to say a single word, not even make a noise. I was exhausted and dehydrated, my head buzzed and my tongue was dry like a piece of toast. I simply nodded.

We got to Doña Toña's house quite late. Following the instructions she had given us, we went directly to the backyard to sleep. Antonio, after boasting about the delicious dish cooked by Doña Toña he'd had for dinner, went to sleep in the opposite corner of the enclosure.

After the exercise, I was very hungry and thirsty. I drank several big gulps of tepid water from the water decanter. My thirst quenched and the cold beginning to seep through my body – the temperature dropped quickly – I couldn't get out of my mind the image of the delicious and warm dish prepared by Doña Toña. The hunger pangs, and having nothing to put in my mouth, pushed me to try the peyote. After all, it was food... I also thought it would relax me and help me sleep. Big mistake.

The freezing wind blew hard in the darkness of that deserted area. We spread the tarpaulin on the floor and covered ourselves with the blankets.

At first, the peyote wedges had a pleasant flavour. They tasted like mushrooms, perhaps slightly bitterer. When we'd had four or five each, we stopped and waited for a bit. We were worried about getting too drugged up. While we waited, my friend told me another one of his stories.

"I'll tell you something very funny. Do you know what I've been doing, lately? Stealing pens."

"Stealing pens?"

"Yes. I steal them in hotels, restaurants, civil servants' offices or banks, I mean: places where usually they have cheap pens to lend to the public and where they aren't always nice to their clients. I ask to borrow one and wait for a bit. When they get distracted, I take it. People usually don't realise and that's my way of paying the system back for the inconveniences it creates for me. When people aren't very kind or take advantage of you, you must react. The lack of reaction makes them become even more abusive. People who never want to fight, never want to confront their enemies, never want to have problems, those are the ones that, ironically, have the most problems of all. You think that if you don't fight, people will leave you in peace. It's a mistake. If there's something I've learned from life is that we have to fight every inch, every minute. That's what prevents future confrontations. We have to ensure that those around us realise that their actions have consequences. No bad act will go unpunished. Sometimes one can't be bothered, you think you should just let it go; that's the way the people who act unjustly grow stronger."

"And what happens if they catch you?"

"That hardly ever happens, and if they catch me, I say it was an oversight: 'Lucky you told me, otherwise I'd have taken it with me. I have the bad habit of keeping all the pens. I'm so absentminded…'"

"Don't they get angry?"

"Nobody gets angry for a simple cheap and bad quality pen. They think it was truly an oversight. Who would think it is part of a plan? However, its absence, although insignificant, can be bothersome. It's an unimportant detail until you get a taste of your own medicine and discover that the little details, like treating people in a friendly and kindly manner, or like having a cheap pen at hand, are important."

"You're bonkers."

"I bought some big jars to keep them. I have a huge amount! All full to the brim!"

I laughed, wholeheartedly.

Half an hour had passed and we didn't feel anything; hence we ate another five wedges of peyote and waited again. Nothing. When we started with the third round we were already tired of its taste. We consumed a new round with a fair amount of effort and reached twenty wedges each.

"I give up. We've tried it and they've had no effect," I said, tired. "My stomach is sickened with so much peyote. I want to sleep."

"Me too."

I lay down and closed my eyes. When I closed them, I saw it: a cactus opened and from inside it another one came out, then another and another. I heard how my friend lay down and anxiety overwhelmed me. If he fell asleep, I'd have to fight all that alone.

Then I heard him ask me:

"Do you see it?"

"Yes, I do," I replied.

From that moment on, we didn't speak again. Each one of us was in the middle of our own surreal dreams. With my eyes closed tight, I flew over the most brightly coloured cacti fields. Then I reached the mountainous areas. I was capable of steering my flight, moving towards one area or another according to my wishes. I managed to go towards a mountain, in particular, zigzagging between the trees, flying under waterfalls and even getting inside the burrows of some animals. The problem was that piloting my flight required an exhausting mental effort. The smaller the place I chose, the more precise my movements had to be. The speed at which I moved was very fast, therefore I had to be very swift and keep well ahead, and that exhausted me.

The flight only took place when I had my eyes closed, so, from time to time, I opened them to rest. The best bit was that when I closed them again I went back to my previous position, as happens when you pause a video.

After a while, I reached the sea. It was the coast of the village of my childhood holidays, and I knew it well. Under the sea, everything was better: the colours were more intense, it was easier to steer my dive, the speed was lower and there was a great sensation of calm. And, inside the sea, there were more things I could enter and explore: deep submarine canyons, prairies of huge seaweed, hollows in the rocks… I spent a bit of time following some small goldfish, and then I joined a group of dolphins. Swimming with the dolphins was very funny; we pirouetted and jumped out of the water. After playing for a while, they took me to the Rock of the Missing. Then they took off and left me alone.

I kept quiet, feeling bewildered. Why precisely there?

I opened my eyes to rest and assimilate the place I'd reached: the Rock of the Missing. The wind, that had been blowing hard all night, had suddenly stopped. Everything was peaceful and quiet. I closed my eyes again and heard a voice inside: 'You must go inside and ask the Dragon your doubts.' I entered the underwater cavern and started diving in a screwdriver's movement. I saw huge sea urchins and phosphorescent starfishes on the walls; I saw brightly coloured crabs. Everything was gorgeous. Then I stopped spinning. I was getting close to a T-junction and I had to choose the path to follow. I heard a voice, again: 'I'm the Dragon. I don't need you to ask me the question; I have the answer. Follow the path of your heart. You must always follow the path of your heart.'

I opened my eyes to rest for another moment. When I closed them again, I was no longer at the Rock of the Missing. I was again in the field of cacti, although now everything was moving slower, and was less bright. Black holes began to appear in the middle of the fields, several hours had passed and the hallucinations were weakening. After a while, I was able to interact with my friend. We laughed excessively, histrionically. The endless belly laughs made our tired eyes weep. The sensation was peculiar because, in contrast to alcohol, I was able to remember absolutely everything. I was also fully aware that I was totally drugged.

Then we heard a noise.

"If an animal attacked us now, I wouldn't dare to kill it."

"Why not?" I asked after I stopped laughing.

"Because I'm drugged and, if I kill it, perhaps tomorrow I'll discover it was a person."

We laughed again.

The noisy animal happened to be Antonio, whom we'd completely forgotten about. He approached us, sleepy.

"Stop making noise, mad *pinches*. You're going to wake up the whole village."

"Antonio, please, I ask you, don't anchor us down to reality, allow us to carry on flying; you're ballast."

More laughter.

The poor man turned around, in a bad temper and left us to it. After that, we tried to speak softer, but I'm not sure we managed. Not being allowed to make noise made us laugh even more.

The dawn arrived and we hadn't slept a wink. Antonio looked angry. My friend's face was that of a crazy junkie: dirty, unkempt hair and vampire eyes where the pupils occupied ninety per cent of the iris. It was like an iris eclipse.

Doña Toña offered us breakfast. I wasn't hungry or thirsty, and I only had some milk to avoid being rude, as she insisted. I felt a great vitality, a pressing urge to jump and run. My brain was in a state of silly happy relaxation; I couldn't help laughing excessively at any nonsense during the whole day. It took me a couple of days to see totally black when I closed my eyes, without any kind of colourful flashes.

Once recovered, we talked about the peyote experience. What I'd seen – or lived that came closer to describing what I had felt – when I was under the influence of the drug had been extraordinary and disturbing and I craved to share it as much as to discover what my peculiar friend had lived.

"What did you talk to Mezcalito about?" he asked me.

"I didn't talk to Mezcalito; I talked to the Dragon."

"Really?" he asked, smiling.

"Yes. The voice I heard asserted it was the Dragon's."

"And what did it tell you?"

"It was all very strange. First, I'd been flying over the cacti fields, and then I got to the sea and went diving. Finally, I reached the Rock of the Missing and entered the underwater cavern. After making some headway, I reached a junction and the voice told me to follow the path of my heart."

"What?" he asked, surprised.

"It told me to follow the path of my heart," I repeated, amazed by his reaction, "but that doesn't mean anything to me. Why do you find it so interesting?"

"Fuck, that's very weird but also funny."

To see my friend so surprised was extraordinarily unusual, and it left me puzzled. I decided to act carefully; I knew if I showed too much interest he wouldn't say anything. I changed the subject.

"Who did you talk to? What did they tell you?" I asked.

"Nothing, nothing, nothing..." he replied, seemingly normal again.

However, I thought I sensed a fleeting halo of sadness in the depth of his gaze. Sadness? That was another unlikely attitude for my friend. What was happening?

Despite my efforts and my insistence, he refused to tell me anything at all. I didn't like that reserve after I had told him my story and it bothered me, especially the matter of the Rock of the Missing because it had remained unfinished business for many years. The thing is that I didn't manage to get my eagerly awaited replies and, in the end, getting angry, I refused to talk about the matter any longer.

Chapter 11. Bad Quique

In the village, there was a boy called Enrique, but nobody called him by that name. His name was Bad Quique. It was a simple nickname and its simplicity gave it its unique impact. It wasn't bombastic or pretentious, like Legbreaker or Dogkiller, it wasn't even Quique The Bad. It was, simply, Bad Quique, nothing more and nothing less. It wasn't necessary to ask who he was bad for. He was bad for you, bad for your health, bad for your friends, bad for your life. He was a brute, strong and cruel; he seemed to have been made to rule with tyranny over the fates of the boys of the village. The boys of his age feared him, the older ones avoided him and he terrified those of us younger than him. To make us panic, even more, he never went alone. He went with a bunch of boys, who showed little interest in poetry and were known as "the Baddies".

The Baddies presided over the lucrative business of joints, pills, coke and heroin. During their working day, they smoked joints and took coke or Es, without anybody daring to say anything to them. The only thing they didn't use themselves was the heroin they sold to the village junkies.

The Baddies' headquarters was near the arcade. The back door of the arcade opened into a park, dirty and neglected. The Baddies lived there; that was their kingdom. The park had two areas: one with a stone bench circled by bushes and the other where there was a much-damaged basketball court. They had the drugs hidden in the bushes. The bench acted as the throne of their kingdom. Sitting there, they ate sunflower seeds, drank beer, used drugs and trained in the use of their butterfly knives, boasting about their skill. The intimidating arsenal was completed by brass knuckles and a baseball bat, which they some-times used to play matches in the park. Obviously, nobody went to that place unless they had a very good reason to; but, unfortunately, the Baddies weren't always at the park. Sometimes you might enter a bar and there they were, drinking beer, Estrella Galicia, smoking and eating their beloved sunflower seeds. They were always pissed off, looking angry, and your appearance created a tense moment. Once they'd seen you, you couldn't run away; if you did, they hunted you down and that was even worse. In such cases, you had to put up with it, bearing their onslaught as best you could. They insulted you, they spit sunflower shells at you and pushed you, but you couldn't confront them or fear them. It required a special art to put up with that avalanche without showing any fear or courage they might consider bravado. Both feelings were punished in the same way. Because, after all, what you were actually doing by turning up before them was to commit a crime. Which one? Bothering them with your miserable and insignificant presence.

At night, when you went fishing for cuttlefish, you would see them getting off speedboats with heavy plastic bundles. Fast, fiery, dark, suspicious. On those occasions, they wouldn't stop and bother you but their threatening gazes made you realise that you were the one out of place.

Fishing for cuttlefish was a big tradition in the village. At night, they were irresistibly attracted by the light. When there was a full moon, they spread all over the estuary; when there was no moon, it was easy to make them concentrate on a specific spot with a light.

The fishermen launched their barges and small boats and sailed to the middle of the estuary with huge spotlights to attract them. A multitude of small lights, like fireflies, lit the dark and quiet summer nights. However, not everybody had a boat. The young and the old usually went to the harbour. We spent the hours next to the dock, close to a big lamppost that attracted the cephalopods in the total darkness of the night. It wasn't like being in the boat, not as exciting, but you caught good cuttlefish anyway.

You were always crammed. The people who got there tried to get as close as possible to the lamppost because the best places were right under it, where the light was brightest. To get one of those, you had to get there very early, before nightfall. The elderly, usually more far-sighted and patient, knew the best places. The rest of us fell into place as close to them as possible, in a furtive way that wasn't always welcome.

Sooner or later what had to happen, happened. The fishing lines of two fishing rods got entangled due to an oversight, to the sea waves or due simply to proximity. Then a fight would ensue. The closest one to the light would complain vehemently, succeeding in making the other one move a little. That caused the stretching of the whole chain. Less than ten minutes later the space in between had reduced again and a new confrontation took place after another entanglement of the fishing lines.

My friend and I loved to go fishing for cuttlefish since we were kids. It was fun and exciting, even if it was only because we left the house late in the evening and went back at night. With time, fishing for cuttlefish reached a new dimension, neither better nor worse than the first, just different. Several summers had gone by and we began to discover new angles: we started to drink. I don't know if our parents found out; but they must have been worried, at least, due to our loss of fishing ability.

We debuted with the *calimocho* [red wine and Coke] with ease and passion. It was cheap and it didn't taste at all bad. A wine carton of the Cumbres de Gredos label cost hardly a hundred pesetas. The two litre Coca-Cola was a bit more expensive. At an age where the budget our parents gave us was only supposed to be used to buy sunflower seeds, ice creams and sweets, we couldn't afford much more than that. To include alcohol in that budget we had to reconsider the inputs and outputs of the small business we called leisure. That was how we learned to compare prices, to seek bargains, to tighten our belts. The *calimocho* taught us the importance of saving, how the business economy worked and the advantages of group investment to secure a common good. If we got together a little more than a hundred pesetas each, we had enough.

The thing of it was that drinking was all very well and good but we couldn't get home drunk. We couldn't go to night clubs yet; we were too young. How could we drink then? And where? Well, there were two great options: to go to a small secluded cove to spend the day there or to go fishing for cuttlefish in the evenings. In both situations, we were hidden from prying looks while we were there and we ensured that our parents didn't see us drunk. At the beach, we had the afternoon to sober up; with the cuttlefish, we got home when our parents were already in bed.

Hiding in a corner of the harbour, with the red lights of the cigarettes lighting up our faces, the bottle of *calimocho* went from one to the other with the nervousness and anxiety of those who do something new and forbidden. The alcohol loosened up our tongues and the most preposterous plans and wishes burst out, unstoppable, from our mouths. We were grown-ups. We were tough males hardened by vice, that held their liquor stoically as if drinking water, or that was what we wanted to believe... Luckily, the drunkenness wasn't too extreme due to lack of money.

During one of our chats, tipsy due to the alcohol and hiding in the harbour's darkness, my friend unleashed the idea.

"Let's steal some traps."

"What?"

"Let's steal some traps. We'll put them on the beach, close to the rocks. That way we'll be able to get our own catch."

I looked at him, astonished; he always managed to surprise me in the end. After recovering from my initial surprise, with the Dutch courage of the alcohol, I didn't think it was too bad an idea. It scared me a bit, but with Dark Shadow gone from the village a few summers ago, we had a clear path ahead. The idea attracted me more than it scared me; therefore I decided to play along, exposing the possible problems that worried me.

"If the fishermen find us stealing their traps, they'll scalp us."

"No, they won't see us; we'll do it at night before they go fishing. And, we'll only steal the oldest and most damaged ones," my friend said, confidently.

"OK, we steal them at night. Where do we keep them?"

"We don't keep them anywhere. We steal them tonight, when the tide is low, we throw them into the sea from the beach and, tomorrow, we come and pick them up again during low tide. We tie them well, we place them at a reasonable distance from each other and that's it. We only need to take the crabs out and fill them up with bait every so often."

"We can't put them on the beach; you already know it's a forbidden place…"

"If somebody sees us diving by the traps, something very unlikely, we'll say we found them there, on the beach. It's impossible for them to prove they are ours; in fact, they aren't. What are they going to do? Arrest some boys for diving near some old half-broken traps?"

The truth was that he was right.

"How will we know where they are? If we mark them, they'll find us and take them from us."

"We won't mark them. We'll tie them all up to a rope and we'll put them in a secluded area, close to the rocks. If there are several and the rope is heavy, they'll weigh enough to not be dragged by the tide. We'll fill them up with bait and we'll dive down and take the crabs out. We do everything diving. You know well how it's done, don't you remember?"

"Yes, I remember perfectly well," I said, half-smiling.

In truth, the plan was very good and the idea of the catch worked as an incentive for me, and I accepted. The odd thing is that it was precisely the project of the traps that gave me the nastiest scare of my life.

That very evening we stole the traps; the tide was low and it fitted in well with our plans. It wasn't difficult. There were innumerable old traps for repair piled up behind the sheds where the fishermen mended their fishing tackle. We grabbed a couple of them each and we quickly rushed to the beach, throwing them into the sea from the shore.

Next day the weather wasn't good. It was cloudy and there was hardly anybody on the beach; that made our task easier. When the tide went down a bit, we couldn't wait any longer and jumped in the water. The traps were there! They had dispersed a bit, but they were all there. We tied them up with a rope, filled them up with bait and separated them, forming a straight lane in parallel with the rocks. Once we'd finished, we stayed contemplating the sea, with the pride of a job well done. Arms akimbo, our heads held up high and with a smile on our faces. Mission accomplished! It was at that moment when my friend blurted the statement:

"I never told you everything about Dark Shadow, did I?"

"What?"

"It was me."

"What do you mean it was you? What did you do?" I asked, frightened.

"Nothing, nothing," he replied, sounding amused.

"Come on, man, we already know each other!"

"That summer, you asked me not to tell you anything about my plans. Do you want me to tell you now?"

"Yes. Well… Do you think I should know?"

"Don't start with your fears and your indecision. Yes or no?"

"Yes."

"About the bull or about the house?"

"Fuuuuck."

He laughed a good while, and finally started talking.

"You must remember I told Dark Shadow where the drugs were, don't you? I imagined he wouldn't let that opportunity to make money pass him by. If the only ones who knew about it were us and him and we had been threatened and were scared shitless, nothing prevented him from getting hold of the drugs. That very night, instead of going home straight away, I went by the leisure centre to talk to Bad Quique.

"Bad Quique? Are you bonkers?" I asked, shocked.

"Yes, Bad Quique. I told him that Dark Shadow was planning to compete with them. I told him he'd started bringing drugs into the village of his own accord, through the cliff behind his house. I challenged him to come with me to see it the next day. At first he didn't believe me, but I finally managed to convince him. Anyway, he didn't have anything to lose by going to check it out. If I had lied to him, he would only have wasted a bit of time and he could take revenge on me whenever he wanted.

"Next day, I went by where the junkies hang out and mentioned that Dark Shadow had good material and he was selling it cheap. Then, I went to pick up Bad Quique and we went to Dark Shadow's house to spy on his movements. We were hiding there when he arrived with the bundles. Bad Quique believed me. In case he had any doubt left, when we were going back we met a couple of well-known junkies. The trick worked out perfectly. What else do you need? Bad Quique was furious, enraged. 'He doesn't know whom he's dealing with,' was the last thing he told me before he left.

"A few days later, the bull died and Dark Shadow went after the Baddies. He was so used to getting his own way that he confronted them and didn't give them the drugs. That was his biggest mistake. You can rob from honest people all you want, but you can't threaten the Baddies. You can't fool around with Bad Quique. They burned down his house and he was lucky nothing happened to him. You know the rest: fire, bells tolling, people discover it is Dark Shadow's house and everybody takes it easy. People didn't really start moving until the fire began to spread to the forest. Nobody went to comfort him; what's more, one could almost feel the elation in the atmosphere. Alone, down on his knees and with the villagers turning their backs on him. A very theatrical image. And what else did he expect? Don't forget that lesson: you can't annoy everybody all the time."

I was speechless. I didn't know what to say and, as it was late, I went back home. I was walking with myriad thoughts in my head. My friend had astonished me. What a pair of balls. If they had caught him, I don't know whose house they would have burned. He was starting to play very hard. Nobody could stop him and danger seemed to stimulate him. It was no longer a matter of being a peculiar individual, or of having a strong personality and feeling confident in himself; it wasn't only a matter of doing funny or ironical things, although that remained still the main goal of his life; it was about taking a challenge to the limit, playing with very serious things, that he treated as a joke. He had destroyed Dark Shadow's life. Did he deserve it? Probably. Did anybody feel sorry for him? Probably not. But that wasn't the issue. My friend was starting to act so coldly that I was scared. It fitted in with his usual lack of concern, but the things he did were getting more and more serious. It wasn't enough to win; he had to do it in a way he found funny or he had to look for an extra challenge. He always walked a step ahead, taking decisions about good and evil, seeking to always get his own way. It was as if he was playing with little children and he tricked them with something simple and evident to enjoy himself, sure in the knowledge that he was far superior to them. I thought again about Dark Shadow and I didn't really feel sorry for him. What my friend had done was wrong, but... But I hated Dark Shadow. That but was the thing that made me unable to totally condemn him. Then, I thought I should be careful. If you look into the devil's eyes for too long you end up becoming the devil.

Chapter 12. The Rock of the Missing

Many lost coves peppered the coast. To reach them it was necessary to go on a long excursion through the forest and a descent, not always easy, to the sea.

The day in question we'd chosen the beach of the Drowned Men, the one closest to the Rock of the Missing. One could reach it thanks to a zigzagging path carved into a very steep hill. You had to hold on to the trees to avoid slipping down, and it wasn't easy when you were loaded with plenty of food and drinks to spend the day on the beach: bread, chorizos, meat pie, water, *calimocho*... The risky descent meant that it was always empty; therefore we were not expecting any company.

When we saw the Baddies, it was already too late. They had also seen us and we couldn't backtrack without it being noticed. Dignity and fear were fighting a battle in our minds and unfortunately, dignity won.

"Shit," I mumbled softly.

We tried to settle as far away from the Baddies as we could, right in the opposite corner of the little cove. The problem was that we were still too close. I don't know what kind of shady deal they were planning, or if they were simply reaffirming their authority, but they decided the beach wasn't big enough for both groups and, given that they were the Baddies, we were surplus. It was very clear, crystal clear.

One of them stood up and came straight towards us. Then he ordered us, bluntly and brutally:

"Out of our beach."

I hesitated for an instant. I didn't doubt if we should stay or leave, rather how to do it without losing too much face. Then he approached me, pushed me and shouted:

"Out of our beach!"

Immediately, I started to pick up the things. I heard laughter and the cheers the rest of the Baddies, Quique included, dedicated to the one who had stood up to threaten us. Then, the temper of my friend, who hadn't bothered picking up any of his things because he wasn't thinking of leaving, came out to play.

"I want to buy cocaine. Do you have any crack to sell me?"

The laughter stopped; they looked at us and weighed the possibility of business. Was it a bluff?

"You don't use that, fucking brat. Imagine if Daddy finds out."

Bad Quique himself had pronounced that sentence. Really scary. I wished my friend would simply nod, let it go and turn around. A voice inside of me kept shouting: 'Don't reply, don't reply.' I would have given anything to be able to leave calmly, without any problems, but I knew it wouldn't be that way.

"There are many things about me that my father doesn't know because I don't tell him. I'm sure the same happens to you. Those things are kept between you and me. Or have you already forgotten Dark Shadow?"

Hard and long silence. All the gazes were trained on Bad Quique, waiting for a reply from the supreme emperor who decides the life or death of the slaves at the Roman circus.

"OK. We'll do some lines together, that way you'll become real men. You're going to pay me five thousand pesetas and I'll sell you half a gramme. I imagine you won't have money, but it's OK, I'm not like the banks and I'll give you credit. After all, I know where you live!"

Belly laughs from the Baddies.

"No problem," my friend replied. "There are road bars, with neon lights, where they charge you far less for turning you into a real man."

Another belly laugh.

"He thinks he's funny. How lucky we are! Shall we carry on with the comedy club or shall we do the lines?"

"How much did you say it is?"

"Five thousand pesetas. No discounts."

"Like these," my friend replied, laconically, producing a huge purple banknote from his rucksack. "I pay cash, as I pay his mother," he added, pointing at one of the Baddies whose mother had a sweet shop.

Another general laugh, except for the son of the said woman, of course.

"Don't you dare mention my mother or I'll rip your head off and I'll piss on it, son of a bitch!" the aforementioned spat out.

"Of course I was talking about the sweets," my friend clarified, an innocent expression on his face.

Bad Quique burst out laughing again, now louder.

"This guy is a comedian!"

The other one reddened and looked at Bad Quique. He was seeking permission to start a fight. Luckily, he didn't get it.

"Enough nonsense," Bad Quique asserted. "We're going to have a therapeutic line and then we'll jump off the Rock of the Missing."

The statement echoed, charged with energy as happens when someone lets out a blunder he didn't mean to say, something one regrets the moment it comes out of one's mouth. Even Bad Quique realised he'd gone too far. We all knew the stories about the Rock of the Missing and we went quiet. The silence increased the tension in the atmosphere. The challenge was out there and nobody wanted to join in. What's more, we all wanted it to be forgotten, but the Baddies couldn't afford to back down and behave like cowards. I thought there was only one option: if I could manage to change the subject and try and smooth things over, perhaps it would all end up as an amusing anecdote.

"Well," I interjected, getting the bottle out. "A bit of *calimocho* to warm up?"

Bad Quique extended his arm, staring at me. He was very close to me; I could almost smell his breath.

He had his eyebrows very close together and his big unibrow hid tiny malevolent eyes. His deep black, long and straight hair, made him look wild. He was very strong and he was very scary. He grabbed my bottle of *calimocho*, which was already his and went back to their shady corner of the beach with his henchmen. It appeared that the danger had passed.

We sat down at the other end of the small cove. It was a worse area than theirs; there was no shade, but we hadn't come off that badly and that encouraged me a fair bit. I swam in the freezing water to try and forget the danger; my friend came with me. We submerged the bottles in the water, holding them under a rock to cool the drinks. After the long bath, it was time to make a fire to cook breakfast. We wrapped the chorizos in tinfoil and we picked at some meat pie while we waited. We had lots of food and we had enough left for an afternoon snack. It looked as if the day was getting better, but it was only the calm before the storm. Shortly after that, the Baddies offered us cocaine; although more than an offer, it was a demand. I was wondering how to refuse when my friend took the floor.

"Give me my half a gramme."

Bad Quique gave him a small bag and my friend handed him the enormous purple note.

"The first one for you and me. My treat. The rest can wait," my friend said.

Bad Quique took his wallet out, poured some of the content over it and divided the white powder into two equal length parallel lines. He did it with the help of a card, with plenty of ability and skill. He snorted one of the lines with the help of a rolled-up banknote and offered the wallet to my friend. He snorted it quite naturally – or so I thought. As soon as he'd had it, he did what I most feared: he challenged Bad Quique.

"Now, you and I will jump off the Rock of the Missing and we'll see if it's true what they say. It's like the owner of a tomato patch: if you want to prove they are good, sometimes you have to fertilise the soil and get covered in shit."

Bad Quique wasn't expecting it. He coughed, cleared his throat a bit and mumbled.

"Bloody brats, they do a little line and believe they're immortal."

"Are you afraid?" my friend asked him, staring him down.

Bad Quique looked him in the eye and challenged him.

"Let's go, brave man. You jump off first, I go next and afterwards your friend jumps off," he ordered, pointing at me.

Nobody said anything else. I was absolutely crushed, frightened shitless.

We swam to the Rock of the Missing, climbed up to it and we looked at the water from the top. We were contemplating fearfully that small dark bottom-less pit and remembered all its legends. The exact place we had to dive into to be able to get out later. Supposing we would ever be able to get out…

"You first," Bad Quique ordered.

My friend closed his eyes and breathed in deeply. He took it calmly, almost overacting. We were beginning to think he wouldn't jump, but right at the moment when Bad Quique was about to say something, he jumped feet down, propelling himself with energy.

It took him eternal seconds to fall into the pit. At least he'd hit the right spot. Then we saw the white foam in the water. And then we didn't see anything else. Some kept waiting to see if he'd appear on that side, but most of us turned around to see if he appeared on the other. We kept looking at the dark sea where he should reappear, that was if he hadn't disappeared for good, of course.

Seconds passed. We couldn't see anything. More time passed and we went from one side of the rock to the other to see if he finally appeared, wherever it might be. Nothing. More and more seconds went by. It had been minutes already. Terror got hold of all of us, even the Baddies.

"He's disappeared. It seems the little faggot hasn't managed to dive deep enough," Bad Quique said, faking calm.

I was so nervous I wasn't able to control myself. In an outburst of rage, I pushed him and insulted him. He turned towards me raising his fist. When he was about to punch me in the face, I heard one of the Baddies shouting.

"There!"

We all looked where he was pointing and saw my friend make his appearance. It was much farther away than we had expected. The route was much longer than we had imagined. He was coughing and puffing. He remained floating belly up for a while to recover. When he did, he managed to swim slowly to the Rock of the Missing and climbed to where we were waiting for him. His eyes were red and his gaze was fierce and challenging. He was smiling in a weird way; it was a bit scary. He faced Bad Quique and challenged him.

"It isn't that difficult. I've already done it; now it's your turn. Disappear and reappear again, like I did."

One of the Baddies asked him what he'd seen down there. The reply was clear and mocking.

"Your friend will tell you straight away when he comes out."

We all looked at Bad Quique. He didn't hesitate. He jumped head first, arrogantly.

Chapter 13. The Tarahumara

We reached Monclova that afternoon. Our destination was the Santiago Apóstol Church, where we had to meet Pancho, the Tarahumara, to pay our debts. The day was hot and dry; the sun scorched and parched the lonely streets of that city of the North of Mexico. The asphalt was on the verge of melting and it burned the thoughtless people who circulated at that time of the day. If that wasn't enough, a blazing wind blew from the North, from the arid and deserted regions separating Mexico and the United States, and that dried the atmosphere even more. The few cars circulating were big old pickup trucks. The men wore Texan hats; they were cowboys out of a Western movie looking like the hard guys of the border.

We had travelled through the big avenues of Monclova to reach the city centre. We parked the car and asked for the church. Some old grannies gave us directions with great kindness and their evident approval: the fact that young people were interested in praying was something they could only contemplate with good eyes. In the vicinity of the church, there was a canteen. We ambled there to have some beers; we were thirsty. When we walked in, we realised that the place was almost empty; there were only two elderly men watching a TV soap-opera with great interest. The waiter was also engrossed in the television and didn't pay us any attention. While waiting for him to serve us, I went to the bathroom to refresh myself. The swing door of that stinking cubicle brought again to my mind the Western movies. Hardly a needle-thin thread of water ran into the dirty sink. Collecting it in the hollow of my hands, with lots of patience, I managed to finally wet my hair and my face. When I came out of the bathroom, the waiter was still watching the telly.

"Sorry to disturb you," my friend said, smiling.

That unpleasant individual still took a long time to serve us. When he finally did, the three small bottles on the bar looked like the adverts for a beer campaign. We drank them up in two gulps and asked for another round; we were thirsty and tired after the long trip in that car with no air conditioning. We were also nervous; we didn't know how the said Pancho, the Tarahumara would be or what kind of work we would have to do to be freed of our debts. The whole business didn't look good.

I had spent the whole trip ruminating about the variety of possibilities we were facing. I had even analysed the option of escaping and going back to Spain; it was unlikely they would follow us all the way there. I rejected it, because the most remote possibility that they might carry out their threats, however unlikely, made it impossible for us to take the risk. We had got involved in this affair ourselves and we would get out of it alone. We had to face it; escaping wasn't an option. Once agreed on that point, I tried to explore the possible different jobs they might make us do. I wanted to know what we were facing, but I had no idea. I had been spinning my wheels, thinking in silence until I felt exhausted. Whatever it was, it had to be something that people from there couldn't do or something very dangerous. It didn't look good at all. Talking to the police was out of the question; they could be even more dangerous and corrupt than the criminals themselves.

Those thoughts kept repeating in my head in a maddening continuous drip the whole trip. Now, leaning on the bar and with a beer in my hand, my fears flowed through my mind like an overflowing stream. I was drinking beer to get some Dutch courage, but I was so nervous it counteracted the effect of the alcohol. When I finished the second round I didn't ask for any more, and neither did my friend, only Antonio asked for a final beer. When the waiter gave it to him and our driver paid, he asked him if he knew Pancho, the Tarahumara.

The waiter looked at us from head to toe and took a few long seconds to reply.

"Who is asking?"

"Some friends he's waiting for," Antonio replied, rather curtly.

"Come back tomorrow evening, around ten," he replied, also curtly.

At two minutes to ten on Sunday, we were again in the canteen. We were finally going to meet the famous Tarahumara. The waiter served us three beers before we had a chance to say anything; his face was serious and unfriendly.

"Yes, the same as usual," my friend said, smiling. "Serve us some tacos, too."

I was incapable of eating. I was extremely nervous and had, once more, lost my appetite. I started to drink my beer while I scanned the place, discreetly. There were hardly any patrons in the canteen, only five people divided into two groups: two old men that looked like retired cowboys and three young boys dressed like rockers. None of them corresponded to the image I had in my head of the famous Pancho, the Tarahumara.

Then, he came in. He didn't look as I had imagined, either. He was a short guy, a weakling, extremely dark skinned, with very long hair. He was wearing a dirty white indigenous shirt, old denim trousers and a pair of weird sandals I'd already seen the Peyote Man wearing – they consisted of a simple piece of a tyre attached to the foot by some leather strips. His feet were full of grime; it was really disgusting. He came straight towards us and introduced himself; his expression that of a naïve and excited child.

"I'm Pancho. Let's sit at that table," he commanded, pointing at the one in the farthest corner.

We followed him, without letting go of our beers. He sat on the only chair there was around that table and with a light nod, he signalled for us to join him.

"Have you asked for something to eat? I recommend the tacos here; they are very tasty."

"We've already ordered tacos, but haven't been served yet," my friend replied. "Do you want us to order some for you too?"

"It isn't necessary, the bartender knows me well."

The waiter arrived with a big bottle of Coca-Cola for the Tarahumara and tacos for everybody. The Tarahumara drank a big gulp of Coke and let go a discreetly satisfied burp.

"You are Pancho. Pancho, the Tarahumara. Are you a Tarahumara?" my friend asked, while he devoured his taco… and mine.

"Yes, I am. Do you know anything about my people?"

"They are an indigenous tribe that live in the Chihuahua Mountains, in the heart of the sierra Tarahumara. They are legendary runners, mythical, tireless. The most unrelenting runners in the world. I've heard about the Tarahumara race, an annual contest very hard and famous."

"That's right," he affirmed, pleased.

"Sorry," my friend interrupted, "I'm going to order more tacos. Do you want any?"

"Yes, order some more. As you well say," he carried on, "we, the Tarahumaras are the best runners in the world. We've been running for thousands of years. Our name is *raramuri*, which means those who run. My people have been hunting animals by pure exhaustion for several generations. We chase them in teams obliging them to make long detours. We keep going for hours, as if it were a relay race until the animals drop exhausted. In that way, from one generation to the next, we've got used to long-distance races. We run with little oxygen in the heights of the big mountains of the Mexican Sierra

Madre. That's how a race of Fierro [Iron], pure superheroes, has been forged..."

"Here come the tacos!" my friend cheered.

The Tarahumara stopped for a moment to eat his taco, then continued.

"As I was saying, we're the best runners, but we started to be ignored, as happened to all the rest of the indigenous tribes. They stole our lands and our rights. We didn't give up and we started to challenge the world with the Tarahumara race. Although many foreigners take part, it's always won by one of ours. That's how my people are; isolated, abandoned to their luck, but very proud. With a unique resistance that astonishes the scientists."

"Impressive!" my friend exclaimed, surprised. "Although I had heard some things, I didn't know the story in detail."

"Well, gentlemen," concluded the Tarahumara, "let's leave history and tradition. I haven't come here to talk about my people, but to talk about business. I've heard you owe a favour to a friend of mine. That friend of mine owes me a favour. I went to school; I was privileged because most of my people don't have access to education. I learned to talk like you, to dress like you, to reason like you. Then I realised it was an imposture and I went back to my roots. The problem is that your teachings got really deep inside of me and I discovered some things I haven't been able to forget. I learned how to be bad, false, greedy, I learned how to cheat. I also learned logic and maths and that's where I wanted to get to. You owe a favour to a friend who owes me a favour. I remember that if A equals B and B equals C, A equals C. Is that correct? You have the key to the formula to make all of us happy and keep us in peace. Now that we're here, you must be intrigued and want to know what you have to do, exactly. Don't worry. It's very easy, I'll tell you."

He looked at Antonio.

"You've already finished your mission. You can go back home."

"Me? Already?"

"Yes. Right now. Our plans are none of your business. If you find out anything else you'll have more chances to die. Do you want me to tell you what I learned about probability at school? Today I don't have the time. Go and don't get into any trouble. If you try to do anything stupid, you and your family will die. Now you know. Pray for the Spaniards to do their job, otherwise, you'll also have to pay for them."

Antonio walked to the door, baffled. At first, he tried to leave quickly, then he hesitated several times. Finally, he went back and shook our hands with affection. He said goodbye in a heartfelt way; it was a wordless apology.

"Good luck."

When he started to explain, the Tarahumara completely changed his tone of voice and the way he talked. He went from talking with passion and vehemence to using a didactic and monotonous tone. His speech turned academic and with no feeling, using unnatural sentences that sounded as if he were reading them out of a book and didn't suit him at all.

He seemed to be repeating a speech learned by rote, like a child in school.

"To the North of Coahuila, on the border with the United States, there's a beautiful natural park: Maderas del Carmen. It includes a semi-desert plain and a mountainous area with a multitude of unique species. The natural park covers an enormous extension. One section belongs to the United States and the other to Mexico, with the Río Grande dividing the two. Although it's monitored by forest rangers, it's difficult to control such a huge expanse. There are no roads and the only way to cross it in its entirety is on foot. That is madness, as it means crossing mountains difficult to get to and semi-desert areas where one can die easily: snakes, scorpions, dehydration, etc. The list of risks is very long. The plan is to cross the river with cattle and take them to the United States. There are many cows grazing in the greenest zones of the park and they are exhausting the bushy areas of a unique ecosystem. They are wild cattle that escaped long ago and have reproduced uncontrollably. The thing is that it is not always easy to recover the animals inside a natural park. The project consists of protecting the autochthonous wild fauna by getting rid of these loose animals. The gringos have the money to take care of such things and protect nature, that's why they are the ones bringing in the money for the project. They'll pay us per head of cattle. We'll sacrifice them in Gringoland; we'll have to cross the border. You will pretend to be Spanish scientists visiting the park to complete a project on the effect of stockbreeding over the local flora and fauna. If they see European researchers it will lend it more credibility. That's how we find ourselves where we are, anything coming from outside is always better. Foreigners are allowed to do things they wouldn't allow a Mexican. Bloody complexes... Anyway, I have all the necessary permits ready, I only need your signatures."

I was stunned and couldn't help but say what I was thinking.

"We aren't scientists! Do you want us to cross the border with the United States using fake permits? They'll throw us in jail. They might even kill us!" I objected, unable to hide my fear.

"There's no problem, don't overcomplicate things. You only have to pretend to be scientists. There isn't anything truly illegal. The forest rangers in both areas and the people of the Migra, the Border Patrol, are aware of the project. You only have to accompany us, cross the border and deliver the cattle to the agreed place. The rest is for us to worry about."

My friend shrugged; we had no other options. He stood up and asked the waiter for a pen. Once we had signed the permits, the Tarahumara collected them and stood up.

"Tomorrow we have a banquet, a big meal before we leave. We'll prepare chargrilled venison; it's delicious," he said, licking his lips. "I'll come to pick you up at midday. Let's meet here."

Without giving us a chance to say anything else, he walked out of the door. Right at that instant, I saw my friend hiding the pen in his pocket. I shook my head. We were in a terrible mess and the crazy fucker had to steal pens.

He winked at me and smiled, excitedly.

"It will be a big adventure."

And indeed it was.

Chapter 14. Go down to check

Bad Quique had jumped off the Rock of the Missing. We peered over to see if he had dropped in the right place, and so it was, there was a trail of white foam right at the centre of the small pool. He'd also hit the right spot. What happened next was a repeat of the same actions as the previous time: they all turned around to see him come out from under the other side of the rock. However, I didn't move, aware that it was my turn afterwards. I stayed alone on the spot of the rock from where one jumped, breathing deeply and trying to prepare myself for what awaited me. I was the next one. I'd have to jump! I felt vertigo and panic just by looking over the edge.

We waited longer and longer. Due to my circumstances, I was less aware of how much time had passed, but there came a point when surprised at the delay, I decided to join the rest and peer over the other side of the rock. We waited anxiously, trying to penetrate the sea with our eyes and see under the surface. The terror returned. What if he didn't come out? But if my friend had managed, Bad Quique had to do it too. He had to do it: he was taller and stronger than him and he was Bad Quique; he couldn't fail.

The minutes passed and he didn't surface. We kept waiting in silence, expectant. Each second hurt.

Nobody could last so long without breathing. An indescribable anguish was slowly taking hold of us. He didn't come out.

"He's been under the water for too long, nobody can last so long; he's disappeared," I said, horrified.

"Shut your mouth, you asshole. Bad Quique lasts that long and much more," one of the Baddies replied with barely contained fury.

We carried on waiting. He didn't come out. Time kept ticking; it was clear he wouldn't surface. We all knew it, but nobody wanted to acknowledge it. Nobody wanted to say anything as if the fact of talking would definitely crack that time-freeze where we were suspended. To open one's mouth would mean to start rolling the film and then we'd have to admit what we didn't wish to admit. Nobody broke the tense silence.

Finally, one of the Baddies faced my friend and shouted at him:

"What was down there, son of a bitch?"

"Go down and check."

Nobody replied. We all remained quiet. Bad Quique had disappeared! He had drowned. He was dead.

He was a bastard who had terrorised us and made our lives miserable, but he hadn't broken a leg, he hadn't gone on a trip, no. We were saying he was dead and those were big words. It was a strange and paralysing sensation; you didn't know how to act, how to feel. The anxiety was about to suffocate your heart and you could almost hear your own thoughts spoken out loud.

Then, little by little, the egotism that resides in all of us came to the fore. Our worry about the explanations we'd have to give started to weigh more than our sadness for Bad Quique. I even thought, relieved, that the situation exempted me from my jump. I would no longer have to jump! I had a few fleeting moments of calm, as brief as it was inappropriate.

Once more, my friend's intervention was providential. With a cold blood that left me speechless, he took charge of the situation.

"We're going," he asserted, with total conviction. "If they ask us, we'll totally deny it. We haven't even been here. If you want, you can report it, because he is your friend. If you try to get us involved in the matter and say we were here, you won't get any joy from that. You might end up in a bigger mess; we can blame you for his death or talk about drugs. Don't imagine that this time they'll ignore the drugs; we're talking about a death. We can make everything more complicated and we'll always be more credible than you are: we are good boys and they know it in the village. And, you're of legal age and we aren't. Therefore, you can tell any version you want, as long as you don't get us involved. We had nothing to do with his death, we weren't even here. Full stop."

Either the Baddies were still shocked or they were pondering my friend's words and thinking what they should do. Whatever it was, and however incredible it might seem, they let us go without a word.

Our journey back was quiet. I was climbing up the slope from the beach of the Drowned to the hill. I was immersed in my own thoughts and anxieties, worries and fears. I kept going round and round in my head over what had happened, the possible consequences, the reactions that would follow. Would the Baddies try to get revenge for Quique's death? How would Bad Quique's mother react? Would she come after us? Would she tell our parents? Would she tell the police? What would our parents say if they found out? Would they arrest us all? Would Bad Quique return from another place, or another time, to wreak revenge on us?

As if he'd heard my thoughts, my friend stopped and gave me a pep-talk.

"You've already heard me down there. Bad Quique drowned. Nobody made him do it, nobody pushed him. It was his idea and his challenge. Full stop. We are in no way responsible for his death. The only thing we have to be grateful for is that he's the one who died and not one of us. The Baddies won't drag us into it, I assure you of that. They'll prefer to give their own version and not mention anybody else. If they incriminate us, we'll tell the truth: they challenged us, they threatened us and they made me jump. They had drugs and knives. I survived and Bad Quique didn't. As simple as that. And, the tide is rising and it will soon erase any trace of our presence at the beach. The only way we'd get into trouble is if we bring it upon ourselves. If our parents discover we've been at the Rock of the Missing, we won't manage to get out of the house for the whole summer. Hence, we'll say we've spend the day at La Garita beach, that's right next door. Everything was normal and we haven't seen anybody all day. Understood?"

I nodded. The pact was sealed. The fear of punishment exceeded the anxiety for Bad Quique's death. However, I had a doubt left. What had my friend seen at the cavern? He hadn't explained anything. My curiosity was a tiny light shining inside my head. A diminutive blinking light surrounded by darkness, not bright enough to catch my immediate attention, but persistent enough to not fall into oblivion. That wasn't the right time to make such inquiries; I thought that later on the right occasion to bring it up would present itself.

Chapter 15. Cabeza de Vaca

We were the first ones to arrive at the property where the banquet was going to take place, although it was still early.

The large ranch located on the outskirts of the city managed to impress us; it looked like a walled fortress. It was surrounded by a big stone wall that rose high – even higher – at the entry, creating an imposing setting. Under it, a pair of huge and heavy metal doors blocked the way. In front of the door, there were two armed men with AK-47 assault rifles – the Tarahumara called those weapons 'goats' horns'. Those thugs looked like the ones in the movies: big, full of muscles, wearing dark glasses and carrying assault rifles. Once we identified ourselves they allowed us in, but only after searching us and checking the whole vehicle. They inspected it thoroughly, inside and outside, looking under the car with a device that consisted of a mirror glued onto a metal bar.

We went in. We were surprised by the elegant, refined and luxurious house, perfectly painted in white, hiding behind those walls. A beautiful bougainvillaea climbed one of the walls coming to rest on the ample porch. Close to it, in one of its corners, there was a barbecue in working order that looked like it saw a lot of use. In front of it, a few metres away, a swimming pool with a blue turquoise bottom and transparent waters invited swimmers on such a hot day. A bit farther away there was an ostentatious riding arena with several handsome horses.

We sat on the chairs laid out on the porch. A waitress, dressed in black and white and wearing a cap, brought us some beers. Then a man appeared. He was plump, short, with his hair slicked down the back. At first, his face looked nice and harmonious; but if you paid attention, he had the slightly inexpressive and artificial look of the people who've had cosmetic surgery. He was probably much older than he appeared. He seemed to be very vain due to his hairdo, his surgically enhanced face and his dress. All his clothes were from good labels and carefully ironed, his shoes shone like a mirror. However, despite that careful and agreeable appearance, there was something in him that didn't give off good vibes.

He came out of the house followed by two armed giants that could only be bodyguards and greeted us with a kind gesture, but he never shook our hands. While his gorillas waited at a certain distance, he walked directly to the barbecue and gave it his whole attention. He talked to us while he had his back towards us, without even bothering to turn around and look at us.

"My name is Juan de Dios Cabeza de Vaca [John of God Cow's Head]. When one is getting the fire ready, one has to do it oneself. The amount and the exact heat of the embers are crucial to roast the meat just right. Then we have to consider the animal's age, its genetics, its feeding. There's also the cut of the meat and the time that has passed since the animal was sacrificed. A lot of minute details that in the end result in a meat that might be regular, good or sublime. Do you enjoy cooking?"

"A lot," my friend replied cheerfully, "but I'm vegetarian."

Cabeza de Vaca turned around, suddenly, and pierced him with a fiery look that didn't correspond at all with the first impression one got of him. That plump guy had an overwhelmingly short-temper. And he was furious.

"I was joking," my friend retorted quickly. "I'm more carnivorous than a liger. Do you know what a liger is?"

Mr Cabeza de Vaca seemed to recover his coolness and turned around again with his back to us.

"Ha, ha." He laughed unenthusiastically. "We have a comedian. What's a liger?"

"A liger is an animal, half lion and half tiger. When I was a child I saw it at the circus. They were advertising it with much fanfare. It had a lion's mane and stripes like a tiger. They said that it had inherited the fierceness of both animals and it ate an incredible amount."

"I studied Veterinary Science," Mr Cabeza de Vaca said. "That crossing of species would be possible, but probably the individuals born of it would be sterile."

"Are you a vet?"

"Yes. My father had a huge ranch and wanted me to study Veterinary Science. I like the animals, especially grilled," he said, laughing. "Do you know what I remember the most from my university years? The teachings of a professor who was a motherfucker. In his first practical class, he got us in a circle and asked us what the most important thing was when treating a sick animal. There were a variety of replies. One girl said the most important thing was to heal the animal; another one stated that improving its wellbeing was fundamental; a third one affirmed that an increase in production was what really mattered. The professor was very clear: 'No. The most important thing when treating an animal is that it doesn't hurt you. The trick is very easy: you place the owners in front of the most dangerous part of the animal. For example, if it is an animal that bites – a dog– the mouth must point towards the owners. Then you can explain the reasoning very convincingly: you tell them it's better it sees their faces to ensure it remains calm. That way you'll make sure you don't get hurt. And, as the owners adore the animal, it will never hurt them as much as it would hurt you.' That's what I have left of my career. That's the most important teaching after so many hours of practice and studying."

"Fascinating!" my friend exclaimed, admiringly. "Do you want me to tell you an anecdote about a job I had? It's the most important thing I've ever learned and it's become imprinted in my brain."

"Let's go; I love good stories."

"I worked on private investments. The people who came to see me were of two types: very pernickety people and weird people. At first, I tried to calm them and reason with them, but it wasn't always possible. There came a time when it was affecting me; I got home burned out. Then, I decided to strike back. I invented the Parable of the Tomato Patch. When somebody told me some boring story, I replied giving them an example, which I invented as I went along, relating what they had told me to a tomato patch. If they asked me about the Stock Exchange, I would tell them: 'It's the same for the owner of a tomato patch; one has to water it every day…' If they told me that some transactions gave more benefits than others: 'It's like the farmer who has a tomato patch, some will grow faster than others…' If they told me that they wanted to reduce their investment on a product: 'It's the same for the owner of a tomato patch, if you don't invest in water and fertiliser, you won't get cherry tomatoes…' If a guy started telling me that lately, he had a strange cough, a sick aunt or a new car, I would tell them: 'The same happens to the owner of a tomato patch…' That way I paid them back for all the madness, boring stories and the earfuls I got and by playing those tricks I felt I was getting even. I considered it a draw. You give me shit and I give you back the Tomato Patch."

"Magnificent!" Cabeza de Vaca clapped. "It's a great idea. I love it! I'm going to start using it for my meetings."

The owner of the house was laughing his head off with my friend. It was evident that they had connected well from the very beginning. The two had a very similar sense of humour, and they were also self-assured and had similar personalities.

I also laughed good-humouredly. I remembered the thing about the Tomato Patch from when we were children. Although I'd always been curious about it, he'd never told me what it was about. What was clear to me was that he hadn't invented it for that job he had mentioned – if he had had that job at all. He'd been using the Tomato Patch trick since he was a child.

"My father was very tough with my education," my friend continued.

"Although I don't know your dad, I'm sure mine was harder. There were quite a few of us siblings and the boys' education was Spartan. He made us get up in the early hours to look after the animals, he made us ride for hours, chase the cattle and shoe the horses, eat little and work a lot. We were the children of a millionaire and our life was harder than that of the house servants; we had to show a good example. He never allowed us to have a hot bath; I couldn't do it until I went to university. During all my childhood I bathed in cold water. We had to behave like true macho men; it builds up your character and makes you strong. If you can overcome it, you know you can overcome anything."

"My life hasn't been easier either, I can assure you," replied my friend. "My father is very similar to yours; I had a very tough childhood. My life was a continuous challenge, a continuous training; they even took me to military boot camps for soldiers and for elite fighters. I understand perfectly well what you mean. I could tell you a thousand stories…"

They moved away from the group and carried on talking and talking for hours as if the rest of us didn't exist. One could see they were complicit, happy, and having fun. By contrast, my day was quite boring; nobody wanted to talk to me. They avoided me. After trying a couple of times I decided it was impossible and gave up, eating apart from the rest. I walked around and drank; I visited the riding arena and observed the horses to distract myself and not think about my problems. Every so often I looked at my friend; he was still very happy, talking to the owner of the ranch as if he had nothing to worry about.

It was getting dark and it was time to leave; the next day we had to get up early to set off on our trip to Maderas del Carmen. Mr Cabeza de Vaca said goodbye to all of us with a slight nod. However, he shook my friend's hand with affection. They both seemed to care deeply for each other as if they'd known one another all their lives.

"If you ever need anything, here I am. I am serious; it's not just something I tell everybody. You have my word."

"Thanks very much. I'll do that," my friend replied.

Reaching the heart of Maderas del Carmen isn't an easy task. Removed from civilisation, getting there is a big adventure in itself. Riding the four-wheel drive with the Tarahumara and a skilled driver, we slowly traversed that deserted area. A huge extension of dry and inhospitable terrain opened up before us. We travelled through mud tracks, leaving behind us a dust trail that disappeared in the distance. We looked back and we could only see that dust cloud.

"It's a quasi-allegorical image; we've burned our bridges and now we sail into the unknown," my friend said, sarcastically.

Because the terrain was flat and monotonous, it looked as if we weren't moving forward. Only some mountains visible on the horizon, which were slowly getting closer, refuted that sensation of immobility. My friend enlivened the trip with another one of his theories:

"You shouldn't talk about your job unless it is to tell a top-class anecdote. When you have a few beers with somebody, you can spit at him, you can punch him, you can even piss on him, but you shouldn't be boring, you must contribute something. I flee from boring people, from people who don't contribute anything. Life is brief, time is gold, you can't waste it with tedious people. Don't boast about the importance of your position; don't give me details of the fights between your colleagues (whom I don't even know); don't explain to me why you deserve a promotion, don't complain about how hard your working day is, talk to me about something extraordinary, tell me something funny or leave me in peace. Don't be grey."

"Not everybody has an interesting job; some jobs are really boring," I objected.

"It isn't a question of the job; it's your attitude towards it. I knew a man with a horrible task: he had to deal with people's complaints. That guy opened a dictionary each morning and looked for a peculiar word: rhinoplasty, pumpernickel, igneous, etc. When it was his turn to listen to an irate, weird or boring person, he played the game of trying to insert his chosen word into the conversation. The more times he managed to include it, the better his score. When his wife asked him how his day had gone, he never told her he had been told-off ten times, he told her he'd introduced the word pumpernickel ten times in the conversation. He was a very funny guy, truly amusing and witty, an inspiration. It's the individual who determines if his or her life is sad or funny. Don't ever be grey."

"I'm not especially funny," I replied, somewhat irked. "I don't usually tell funny or very interesting stories."

"That isn't true. You are funny in your own way. Your seriousness is funny. It's as if you were pretending to be serious. Your shyness prevents you from bringing out the good in you. On the other hand, you accept jokes in good humour and that's a rare virtue too. People like to play jokes on others, but they usually aren't good sports when they're on the receiving end. Our friendship has always been based on the same principle: you are good, responsible, and I make it my task to bother you and push you to the limit. And, there's something else in you that I haven't found in anybody else: you are a magnet for attracting weird people, crazy individuals and the most unexpected problems. That livens anybody up and turns your friendship into a treasure. We complement each other. One of us had to be intelligent and a good person and it was your load. I had no other option but to be funny."

"You know that's not true. You're very intelligent," I said, smiling.

"That means I'm not a good person, because you haven't defended that."

"It depends…"

"Very Galician [Galician people are expert in the art of question dodging]," he replied, amused.

The car was still progressing slowly. Once we got closer, we were impressed by the mountains. They created a huge barrier due to the substantial difference in their height with respect to the plain through which we were travelling. We reached the bottom of the mass and got ready to go up a hill that appeared less steep and inaccessible than the rest. A winding rocky path that seemed only good for goats climbed up that steep and sharp ravine.

As we went up, the path kept getting narrower and steeper all the time. The speed of the four-wheel drive progressively slowed down, until, driving in first, we were hardly moving any faster than somebody on foot. The driver's skill deserved some praise. With his head and half of his body out of the car to check where he was going, he carried on driving through a place I wouldn't have dared to try with an off-road motorcycle. The car leant to one side and the other, like a vessel adrift in a stormy sea. The numerous gaps and stones in the narrow path complicated matters even more.

We only had one last bend left and we'd reach the top, having already surmounted the steep gap. I thought we'd already done it, but the best was yet to come… At the bend, the path became so narrow that the four-wheel drive didn't fit in its entirety. On the right side there was a huge precipice; on the left, a wall. The only way to keep going was to cling to the wall, but the way ahead seemed too narrow for the car.

"We can't get through," I complained, scared.

"Don't worry," said the driver, "we always come this way. The Tarahumara will sit by my side. You two," he said, addressing us, "the only thing you have to do is to also cling to the side opposite the precipice. Sit one on top of the other. We'll load all the weight of the jeep on the side farthest away from the void; that way it will be more difficult for it to become unstable and fall. In any case, fully open the windows; if we fell down you would be able to get out and would avoid going over the cliff inside of the car."

I was sitting in the back right seat, on the side of the cliff. I looked down and was terrified. 'What's the advantage if, when the car goes over, we get out of the window?' I thought. The only difference would be that we would roll down the cliff outside of the car instead of inside of it, but our death would be equally horrible. Even with that, I opened the bloody window before sitting on top of my friend. The tension was evident. The driver made the car cling to the wall as much as he could; he folded the side-mirror to get even closer. While a sensation of weightlessness and vertigo flooded us, the four-wheel drive crawled. I couldn't see where the wheels on the right side landed, but I had the sensation they didn't fully touch the ground. I could only see the void below us. The car scratched the wall hard, making a muffled screeching noise in its attempt to claw a few millimetres back. It was the noise somebody holding on to life with steel claws would make.

There was a moment when the wall protruded a bit, a few centimetres that, inevitably, pushed us even farther towards the precipice. Then, at that last moment, the four-wheel drive wobbled and the tyres that were peering over the abyss skidded. We felt how the tyres spun, unable to get traction until the terrifying noise of the landslide came. Huge rocks smashed to bits, exploding in a never-ending fall. The driver lifted his foot from the gas pedal slowly and we were motionless. We felt a swaying sufficiently noticeable to make us grasp that we hung in a delicate balance. Our lives were being weighed in the deadly scales the vehicle had become.

"Don't move at all," whispered the terrified driver.

Chapter 16. The Training

We went back to the village feeling anguished after Bad Quique's disappearance. My friend suggested we should go for a wander before going back home. I was terrified at the thought of facing my parents' eyes, so I accepted. We went to a quiet area: behind my house, there was a road that took us to a small vacant lot surrounded by trees, the perfect place for a chat. We sat there and he started calmly talking to me.

"You know my father; he's a guy with a very strong personality, very self-assured. He's always supportive, helpful, but my father wasn't always like that. I never met my grandparents on my father's side, or my uncle, my father's brother. My uncle died when he was very young. It was in an accident, I don't know for certain what happened. When my uncle died, my grandmother went into a deep depression and ended up committing suicide. My grandfather couldn't cope with the deaths of his son and his wife. He died shortly after, everybody said due to grief. In summary: my father was left all alone. He was eighteen, the whole world fell on him and he hit rock-bottom. One day, he went up to the roof to jump off and put an end to his suffering. When he was on the rooftop, rocking before the void, suddenly a feeling of wrath overtook his body. The fury rushed from his chest to his head, from his shoulders to his fists. At that moment, between life and death, he clearly saw that everybody had abandoned him to his luck and he would live. The rest of the people had been soft and self-centred; they had abandoned him and that wasn't fair. His brother had died in an accident; the rest had been killed by their minds and their own weakness. He wouldn't be like them; he would survive and wouldn't be weak ever again. Things happen; events take place and cannot be changed; the only thing you can do is decide how you'll cope with them. Either you bury your ghosts or they will bury you. From then on, he focused on strengthening his character, putting himself to the test all the time. The objective was simple: turn himself into somebody totally immune to psychological pressure, to despair, to anguish, to sadness and to self-compassion. He started to notice that people are weak when they have to face the games their own minds play on them. That solidified his determination. People underestimate the power of a resilient, imperturbable and effective mind, independent from the problems around it. The mind controls the body and the triumph of the first over the second must be constant. What's more, the mind has to be sufficiently powerful to be able to stop in its tracks when it is trying to destabilise itself. If you can manage to control that, you will not only be happy, but you'll also have a very valuable weapon to confront the world. If you can dominate it, not only will you be able to overcome adversity, but you will also have the capacity to counter a psychological beating, you'll counterattack. An imperturbable mentality guiding an obedient body. It's not a matter of creating a muscular body, but somebody determined and assured. It's something more psychological than physical. Do you understand?"

I didn't know what to say and only nodded. Then he carried on.

"This lecture I've just given you, my father has been repeating it to me since I was a child. I know it by heart. With this philosophy, he educated my brothers and me. Following this doctrine, he trained us morning, evening and night. The tests were continuous. One of them consisted of me lying face up on the floor and my brothers lying on top of me. With their combined weight on me, I felt as if they were crushing me and I was suffocating as if I couldn't get any air inside of my lungs. If I cried, I got anxious and things got even worse. I had to control my panic and my anguish. I had to relax and start breathing slowly, unhurriedly, taking slow and deep breaths. When I was capable of controlling it, I no longer suffocated. Then they would stand up. Test conquered. I had overcome the fear and the anxiety. Another test was about defeating the mentality of the group. My father made an alliance with my brothers and they'd change the glasses from one of the kitchen cupboards to another. They put them in a different location to the usual one. When I asked them where the glasses were, they told me they were in the same place as usual. I would tell them it wasn't true, but he would ask the others and they replied that they were where they'd always been. So serious and sure of themselves they sounded, that you ended up doubting yourself. That was not right. If you accepted their version, they changed them again the next day. You had to stay unwavering to pass the test. Other times, he'd agree with my brothers and tell me my hair was weird. They would all look at my hair every time we crossed paths. They'd keep doing that the whole day. You had to ignore it and appear indifferent. He also had tests on negotiation. He'd contradict you on something you wanted. He would turn your life into hell until you voluntarily accepted his position. In the end, he would sit down with you; he was affectionate and would serve you a big plate of your favourite dish. While you finished eating, he tried again to win you over to his position. You had to refuse again. If you accepted, you had fallen into his trap and shown your weakness, then he'd start defending what you had been defending before and he was attacking. And it would all start again. Sometimes he made us tell him what we'd done during the day and obliged us to include the telling of a small lie. The point was to detect the lie and distinguish it from the rest. These were his teachings about body language. At the end of each lesson, he always explained to us the mechanisms and tricks, the methods and reasons for each test, the different actions and its explanations. That way we learned, from very young, negotiation techniques, body language, to control our fear, anxiety, fury and suffering. We learned to be strong, to ignore pressure, to detect lies, to manipulate the mind. We learned to control the weakness and fear of others, to hide our own weaknesses. My father is sick in the head; I've had a very tough time. One thing is talking about it and another living through it. I've only given you a few examples; there were thousands of different tests, each one harder than the last.

Nobody knows anything about what I've told you because he makes us keep what he calls 'the Secret'. He tells us it is to avoid people knowing our 'powers'. It's a lie. The truth is he knows that if people knew his methods, he'd end up in jail. Someday I'll tell you about Thailand and the Muay Thai, or the story about Melilla and the Foreign Legion. Now it's done and I don't resent him. I wouldn't go through it again; the process to get those superpowers is too painful. It's so hard that, even once you have them, you can't say they're really worth it. But you have them, that's a fact. If you don't think about the past, there's no doubt that having them is cool. He himself taught me not to complain. And, and this is important too, on many occasions his advice and training have been very useful. Today they've saved my life, without any doubt."

When he finished talking, we realised it had got too late. Suddenly, I felt as if I could die of cold and tiredness, too many emotions for a single day. We said goodbye quickly. When I no longer saw him, I set off running. I would get home very late and they'd kill me. The anxiety took over me and the pangs of everything that had happened echoed inside my head. The death of Bad Quique, the madness of my friend's father… And on top of that, I was going to get home late! My parents would be worried; I'd get a big telling-off and many questions I didn't want to answer.

When I got home, things went as I had expected. My parents were waiting for me in the sitting-room, sitting on one sofa each. I tried to pretend normality and calmness, but I was still breathless from my race and made distraught by fear. I stopped dead in the middle of the sitting-room. Their faces had a serious expression. They stopped reading the books they had open and scanned me from head to toe.

"You are very late. We were worried!"

"Where have you been all day? Do you think you live at a hotel? You leave at nine in the morning and don't turn up until eleven at night!"

"We went to the beach to roast some chorizos..." I replied, shyly.

"Have you been at the beach until eleven? Which beach did you go to?"

"When we came back from the beach we went somewhere around to have a snack with the food we had left."

"What do you mean by somewhere around? Who with? Why didn't you come home first?"

"We got talking and it got late... We thought we'd finish earlier, that's why I didn't say anything. I'm sorry..."

"Because you haven't had enough time to talk during the whole day and because tomorrow you won't see each other again, that's why you had to stay talking until eleven. But you already spend together ten hours a day, every bleeping day! What was that crucial matter you had to talk about?"

"Nothing... Our nonsense... About fishing..."

"Well, you'll stay home tomorrow, all day without going out, that way you'll be able to think about nonsense, the sea and the fishes."

I didn't want any more trouble and I accepted the punishment without even trying to defend myself. I had replied just what I had to and had avoided the question I wanted to avoid. I only wanted to go to bed.

"You don't look well. Did anything happen?"

"No. I'm just cold, that's all."

"Of course! You're only wearing your trunks until so late and then you have to pay the consequences."

"And which beach did you go to?"

"What?"

"Which beach did you gooooooo to?"

"Ehhhh, we went to La Garita," I said as I walked away.

"Weren't you going to go to the beach of the Drowned?"

"Yes...but...we changed our minds," I murmured, without turning around.

I left quickly. I locked myself in the bathroom and had a long shower with boiling water. Everything crowded in my mind. I was an idiot. Because I had been late, the matter of the beach had come to light during the interrogation; otherwise, it would have gone unnoticed.

When I came out of the bathroom I felt truly poorly. I went straight to bed. Despite the hot water I still felt cold, really cold. I threw a blanket on top of my bed, got under it, covered myself up to my ears and curled up. Although I wanted to sleep, it took me a while to do it. What had happened during the day kept going round and round in my head. I tried to analyse each action and its consequences. I kept thinking about how to solve each new problem that occurred to me. What if the Baddies snitched on us? And if Bad Quique wasn't dead? What if they told my parents?

The night was horrible; I had a fever and nightmares.

Next day I felt terrible, and I stayed in bed. The fever lasted for several days. The nightmares continued. In the few moments when my fever came down, thoughts about the matter would start going round and round in my head and I would get worse again. I dreamed of drowned people floating in dark waters, lit by spectral lights. In my nightmares, I drowned and travelled endlessly through the underworld.

When I started feeling better, the doubts began eating away at me. Due to my illness, I didn't know anything about what had happened outside of my four walls. I didn't know what had happened about Bad Quique's disappearance, I didn't know what the police might be investigating, I didn't know if anybody had talked too much, I didn't know what the Baddies might be planning to get revenge. I didn't know anything at all! That's why, when the doorbell of my house rang and I could hear my mother talking to my friend, I felt fear and joy at once. Finally, I'd learn something!

They came into my room together. My mother couldn't help herself and seized the opportunity to include him in the scolding for having arrived home so late the day I became ill.

"There you have him: in bed with a fever for several days. You probably enjoy the suffering you make us endure. You are far too old for this kind of thing. You want us to trust you and then you can't behave responsibly. You arrive home late and without letting us know, stay wet after going to the beach, catch a cold and get sick. And who suffers for it? Your parents, who have to stay home looking after you."

"The same happens to the owner of a tomato patch," my friend replied.

"What?" my mother asked, somewhat annoyed.

"Yes. It's the same as if you had a tomato patch. If you water it too much, the plant rots and doesn't produce tomatoes. If you don't water it enough, the plant dries up and it doesn't give tomatoes either. What I mean is, we must learn to provide the right amount of water for it, and that takes time. We have to look after the tomato patch. You, our parents, have given it to us in perfect health and expect us to rise to the occasion, but we are clumsy and inexperienced. We learn from our mistakes; I guarantee you that this time we've learned our lesson. We won't get home late again. I promise you."

My friend had adopted a posture of profound submission and sadness, of sincere repentance. His eyes, very open, shone as if he were getting emotional. His arms, extended, seemed to be asking for a hug. My mother watched him closely for a few seconds. At first, she thought he was pulling a fast one on her; then, for a few seconds, she hesitated; eventually, she decided he was being honest. 'He's a bit odd, but the poor boy seems contrite,' I imagined she must have thought.

"Well, boys, I'll leave you alone. I'll take the chance to go shopping. I'll be back in half an hour. Be good."

We both nodded.

As soon as my mother left the room, my friend winked at me, smiling. That comforted me a bit and made me feel calmer, while I waited to know more about what had happened. We couldn't talk about the pending matters yet, as my mother was still in the house picking up the last few bits and getting the shopping trolley ready.

My friend started talking.

"Yesterday I met some friends who were coming back from the cinema. They loved the movie, although right now I can't remember the name. It was about a couple who met at a restaurant. Both of them were waiting for somebody, but their respective dates didn't turn up. The thing is that, in the end, they end up having dinner together and they have a great time, but they can't become a couple because he's about to get married to his girlfriend from childhood (who is a very bad person) and she has a boyfriend too (who is even worse). In the end, just before getting married, they both leave their partners and they meet again at the restaurant where they first saw each other. Right there and then there's a priest having a meal, who officiates the wedding... It looks very good; when you're feeling better we could go watch it."

I looked at him, surprised. What a rubbish movie! And on top of that, he'd told me the ending!

154

My mother was still at home. My friend looked at me and offered me a knowing smile.

"Do you know what's TFST is?"

"No," I replied.

"It's 'Talking For the Sake of Talking'. It's what one does in these kinds of scenarios to pass the time and bring normality to the proceedings. You want people to see you talking normally, that makes them believe you aren't nervous and you aren't planning anything. You do it without paying attention to it; you talk without putting any thought into what you're saying. You can even ask questions, no matter what the replies are."

"OK, stop with the stories," I ordered him when I heard my mother closing the door of the house. "Tell me what has happened these days."

"Well, well, now don't you rush me. It seems that the big man has been so afraid he's decided to hide in his den, getting out of the way and letting the rest of us clean up this mess."

"I've been ill. It wasn't an excuse, I didn't make it up. I've had a very high fever; I must have caught a cold when we were talking."

"I believe you," he said, after looking at me straight in the eyes for a while.

"Are you going to tell me or not? My mother won't be long. Don't start on one of your long stories. Get to the point and give me the headlines for once, shit!"

"OK, OK, there we go. I'll summarise it as much as I can. The day after…you know what, the first thing I did was to go for a wander with my bike. I went by the door of the Guardia Civil [literally, Civil Guard, a Spanish police force working mostly in rural areas] station and I didn't notice anything peculiar. I walked around the whole village and I didn't meet a single one of the Baddies. As I didn't want to think of anything, or meet anybody, I went fishing. At midday, when I was going back home to have lunch, I saw one of the Baddies. He looked at me sideways and didn't say anything. I noticed – it's true – he was scared and insecure. I only greeted him with a slight nod and he did the same. Nothing happened that afternoon either; in this village, one would have known straight away. On the third day, as I was at the grocery store, I head Paqui of the Ramallos talking. That old woman, who is a professional nosey-parker, was talking about Bad Quique with another old woman. I translate, because you know she speaks in a very thick Galician accent," he said, and started to imitate her in a mocking voice.

"'You know what they're saying about Reme's son. He hasn't turned up for several days.,. He's always been bad news... He was very involved with drugs... And when you get into that kind of thing... Bad, very bad... He made lots of money... And went around the village boasting in his sports car. He, in a sports car! When they had nothing at home... His father was a sailor, but he started drinking and gambling. They say he lost his boat on a bet. Then he started working as a road sweeper. They teased the poor boy since he was very young. He was ashamed because his father was a road sweeper. One day, his father couldn't bear it any longer and left. His mother said that they had made him leave, that he owed money, but I have a suspicion it was an excuse not to have to tell him the truth: that

156

he abandoned her and the boy… And I'm not talking for the sake of talking; she didn't report his disappearance either… We never heard about him again… The mother was left to bring up the child alone. The boy turned up to be rebellious and then came the drugs and the bad company…and that's how he's ended up as he has, missing, like his father… Poor Reme… Abandoned twice. What a shame. You spend your life working and putting up with a drunken husband and a dealer son, and that's how they thank you for it… Will she report it this time? Because I have the feeling that this time they've killed him… I'm telling you this in all honesty. While the father seemed to have run away; I find the son's disappearance stranger. He had his friends and his contacts here and he knew the cove. A brat like him doesn't manage away from here; it's like a fish out of water… They'll eat him up in two minutes. And the drug people don't joke about… People don't talk about it, they don't dare…'"

"Fuck!" I interrupted, annoyed. "I've told you to go straight to the point and stop going round the houses. Tell me what's happened once and for all!"

"I'm already telling you. If you interrupt less, I'll finish sooner. The thing is that they haven't found Bad Quique yet. He's missing."

"Haven't they found him? That's impossible! He must be there!"

"There? Where is there? There, by the Rock of the Missing; only we know where he is. The rest don't know and they haven't gone looking for him there. Well, it's best that I tell you little by little; when I get ahead quickly you interrupt me and it's worse."

He seemed to be enjoying my anguish. The bastard was looking at me and smiling, chilled like somebody who has a fish in the boat and knows it can't escape. My mother came in right then. I hated my friend for being such a pain telling anything, for being so deliberately slow and for not having told me everything he knew – I assumed he knew something else. I cursed him: his calmness had made us lose precious time and the chance to talk.

My friend said goodbye. There wasn't much point in TFST with so many things pending. I was more intrigued, scared and anxious than before he had arrived. With friends like him, who needs enemies?

Once more, I didn't sleep a wink.

Chapter 17. The Legionnaire. Río Grande

In the middle of that natural park, nobody would come to rescue us.

We were trapped in the four-wheel drive, on the edge of the precipice. The car was balancing, about to drop. We couldn't get out through the windows on the inside of the car because we were totally stuck to the wall. We couldn't leave through the windows on the outer side because we'd fall down the abyss. The car had become a death trap, precariously held in balance. We were dumbstruck, holding our breaths as if our breathing would be enough to topple over the car and put an end to our lives.

"Break the back window, we'll get out that way," my friend said. "They'll have to break the windscreen."

Breaking a car window isn't as easy as it seems, especially if you have to do it without moving, to avoid disturbing its balance. I hit it with the handle of the knife my friend gave me. Luckily, the handle had a metallic bottom and after several attempts, the window gave.

I was sitting on top, and I was the first one to get out. The car moved and I fell to the ground on my head. I was out! Next, my friend passed the knife to the guys in front. The Tarahumara broke the windscreen and got out by crawling over the hood. The car rocked again, this time more noticeably until it lost its balance completely. My friend propelled himself and, with a big jump, managed to get out a second before it went over the cliff. The driver was neither as agile nor as quick. At first, we heard a horrible scream; afterwards, we could only hear the noise of the vehicle bumping onto the rocks. By the time it finally reached the bottom of the precipice and stopped moving, the car was totally destroyed.

My friend looked at the smashed-to-bits jeep and then stared at me.

"Oooopa! I escaped by a hair's breadth."

The Tarahumara was still looking at the busted jeep.

"Nobody would be able to survive that. We must carry on and reach the village; we have a long walk left. You must show me everything we've managed to save; even the things inside your pockets could be useful."

We tallied what we had. Apart from the knife we'd used to break the glass, which had finally been left in the Tarahumara's hands, we only had our wallets, keys, belts and a few coins. Not a single drop of water or food, everything had gone over the cliff.

"You've mentioned a village. Is it far?"

"No. I could get there tomorrow morning. The problem is the lack of water; you're not used to it... Well, let's not waste more time. I'll think of something. Follow me."

He set off, walking very fast, without waiting for us. We looked at each other and followed him quickly before he got even farther away.

At first, it didn't look that difficult. I tried to keep my own pace to avoid exhausting myself and having a repeat of what had happened to me with Doña Toña's nephew and the peyote incident. Despite that, after a while, I started lagging behind. I puffed; it was impossible to follow them. They were getting farther and farther away, therefore, I whistled loudly to attract their attention and managed to make them stop and wait for me.

"I can't keep up this pace. We don't have any water and I sweat a lot. I'm dehydrating," I said, gasping for breath.

"We must carry on. When we've advanced a bit more, we'll reach an area where we can get water."

The promise of water gave me renewed energy and I started walking again with vigour. Unfortunately, it didn't last very long and after a short while, they left me behind again. I think we must have been walking for around four hours when they stopped for the first time. We were next to some cacti. The Tarahumara made a cut into one of them and gave us a drink. It tasted pretty bad, but I had really dry lips, my tongue was coated and my throat burning, hence I drank without complaint. Once we had finished drinking, he ordered us to have a rest.

"Wait for me here, and don't move. The sun is low and there isn't long left until nightfall. Lie down and look for a bit of shade; the cacti can help you. Don't move. We'll wait until night-time to start walking again."

He left us resting and went to inspect the surrounding area. As soon as he was gone, I took the chance to talk to my friend.

"How the fuck can you manage to keep up with that guy's pace?"

"Did I never tell you about Thailand?"

"No."

"My father sent me to Thailand when I was little. I went to a training camp for elite fighters. They woke us up at five thirty in the morning. We had to run for hours before breakfast. Afterwards, we had to train: endless series of abdominal exercises, push-ups, kicking canes to strengthen our shins, exhausting sessions of jumping rope, fighting each other... Training, training and more training. The whole day was a continuous training. We hardly ate. I was the only westerner at the camp. It was an inconceivable training for someone not born there; no European would have borne it. Not even the Thais were able to bear it. My father likes history, loves Sparta. He enrolled me there because he thought that training camp was the closest to the apogee, the Spartan educational system, where the boys were removed from their families to train, fight and get tough..."

My friend interrupted his chatter; the Tarahumara was back; he had something in his hand. The sun went down and the shadows finally conquered the desert.

"Have this. It will help you regain your strength and run faster."

'I can't even walk and this guy is talking about running? Is he mad?' I thought.

When he gave it to us, we saw it was peyote.

"Peyote?"

"Do you know it?"

"We've had some experience with it..."

"Well, then you know about it already. Chew it well and eat it."

We ate three segments, one after another. We were going to have the fourth one when he stopped us dead.

"Don't eat anymore. It's only to give you strength."

We waited for a bit, in silence. I was too tired to talk.

"Close your eyes. What do you see?" the Tarahumara asked, finally.

I closed my eyes and saw bright lights.

"Do you see it?" I asked my friend.

"Yes," he replied. "I see it too."

"Then you're ready. Let's run. Start slowly. Follow me."

We started running. At first, I found it hard because I was cold and somewhat dizzy, and felt slightly nauseous. After a bit, everything changed: I felt no longer cold, thirsty or hungry. My bodily sensations disappeared, taking with them my tiredness. My body no longer weighed anything and I felt as if a boundless and endless energy filled my legs. I felt no pain. I was jubilant and could have run for hours without a break. I wasn't being left behind any longer. We were running in a row, more to keep the order than due to lack of energy. The Tarahumara was a few steps ahead, then I, and my friend closed the group. My eyes were capable of seeing perfectly in the moonlight. My senses were sharpened. I noticed the cacti and the rocks before I was fully aware of them as if I sensed where they would appear. I avoided them with surprising agility. My breathing was regular and calm; it created an internal noise that set up the pace and kept me calm.

Although the march lasted a long time, I didn't even notice it. I was feeling very good; I was happy. I had hardly realised the sun was rising already; I noticed the sun rays and everything looked beautiful to me. The sun, big and comfortable, rose majestic over the desert. It looked so beautiful I became emotional, and a tear peaked out of the inner corner of my eye. The speed my legs conferred to my run made the tear stream down my cheek and fly in the wind. I looked back and I saw it disappear in the distance. The sun rays lit it and I could see, for an instant, the rainbow inside. The world was a calm and nice place, all creatures loved each other. From the distance, I saw the adobe houses that made up the village. They were approaching us at full speed.

We got there quickly. We stopped a few metres from the first house we found.

"We've arrived."

"I want to carry on running," I protested. "I'm not tired yet. I'm enjoying it so much I don't want to stop."

"You can't. You must stop and drink water, or you'll die."

"I wouldn't mind dying and becoming one with this wonderful desert."

My friend grabbed me by the shoulders and turned serious.

"We have to drink."

I did what he told me; there was no other option. We went to one of the houses and entered. The owner gave us milk just out of the goat. I wasn't very thirsty, but I felt that it went into my body with ease. It was lukewarm. I noticed its journey inside my body. I drank a whole litre. And then another.

"Now go and have a shower. That will completely dispel the effects."

"Can't we wait a bit? I'm happy like this."

"In the desert one must have a shower early in the morning. If you wait, the sun will heat the pipes that collect the water from the well and you won't be able to do it, it will be boiling."

By midday, most of the effects of the peyote had disappeared and I was able to eat a bit of meat. After resting for a little while, we were ready to receive instructions about what we had to do. I felt strong and relatively calm. I'd need it for sure...

Once we'd recovered, we went for a walk around the four adobe houses in the hamlet. The Tarahumara introduced us to the few people who lived there, all runaways, hiding from the law. The village was far away from everywhere, but only a few kilometres distance from Río Grande, so if anybody went to the hamlet, they had to follow the small tracks of desert sand: slowly and raising lots of dust. They always saw people coming towards them with enough notice to cross the border and be untouchable. Anyway, who'd go there looking for them? Neither the budget nor the eagerness of the Mexican police went that far. Because of all that, the hamlet was in a prime location for anybody who wanted to hide from the law.

"What do these people live off, all year round?"

"Shady deals mostly, the border is very near and very tempting. They also work as firefighters in the forest for the United States, when there are fires on the other side of the river. There are even some shepherds. There's a man who lives permanently in the desert looking after a herd of goats. He only has his animals, a barrel of water and a tarpaulin. He comes to the hamlet every few months, leaves the goats here and goes for a couple of days to the nearest city. There he gets drunk, picks up a couple of whores and then goes back to his beloved desert; that's how he is."

I observed the people of the hamlet; they looked really hardboiled. They were all very dry and frugal with their words as if the desert had shown them that one should waste neither energy nor saliva without a good reason for it. The sun had parched their throats and feelings; had hardened and tanned their souls and gazes. Denim trousers frayed by use, bowed legs, high boots and dusty shirts. Tough guys, capable of doing anything to survive.

When we were left alone with the Tarahumara, my friend confronted what we were all asking ourselves.

"And now what? What's the plan?"

The Tarahumara replied, while looking at the horizon:

"We'll have to wait until the cattle arrive; they should be here in a couple of days. Until then you can do whatever you like."

My friend thought we had to keep ourselves entertained with something, that way time would go faster. One of the village outlaws was repairing the porch of his house, nailing a few sticks, as a makeshift roof, over a wooden structure. They were the trunks that came from the agave plant; I'd already seen them in the desert.

We approached him and offered him our help and he agreed. I collected the sticks from the ground and passed them on, my friend held them together firmly and the Mexican nailed them close together, one next to the other and then he carefully cut them to make sure they were all the same length – *mochando parejo*. The man was fully concentrated on his task and didn't say a word; my friend and I respected his silence. We spent a long time working before he decided to talk to us.

"Where are you from?"

"Spain."

"Where in Spain?"

"I'm *gallego* [Galician] my friend replied."

"Pure *gallego*? *Purito menso*? [Gallego also means stupid in Mexico]," he laughed, amused.

"Not in that sense. I'm from Galicia, in the North of Spain. Do you know our country?"

"My father was Spanish, from Badajoz; he fought in your Civil War."

Then he started talking compulsively as if during his previous silence he'd been accumulating his words, and now they set off, running amok.

"Do you know anything about the Legionnaires? My father was one of them and he always talked about the Foreign Legion with pride. He taught me all their songs as a child; he would never stop singing them when he was happy. He told me that during the war when he wasn't a Legionnaire yet, his battalion got stuck. They'd ordered them to take a post, but it wasn't easy because the enemy was barricaded on top of a hillock and they had no cover at all if they tried to get near. They couldn't surround them and they couldn't keep moving forward either.

"Then, a battalion of Legionnaires, singing at full volume, arrived. My father and his friends smiled; they wanted to see how the famous Legionnaires would solve the matter. They didn't say anything, simply set off and advanced on the enemy trenches. They did it singing, without running or shooting but kept walking steadily. Many fell, but others arrived and shot the frightened men barricaded there who surrendered immediately. The Legionnaires turned around, collected their dead and wounded men and, as if it were the most natural thing in the world, reported back to the command.

"My father was so impressed that he decided to become a Legionnaire immediately. You can't defeat someone who isn't afraid of dying... That's how we are here. A race that has died, it has sold its soul to the devil. This is our hell and our penance. We are the plebeians capable of embracing death itself, we miss it so. We survive because we don't know how to do anything else. Life here is so hard that by dying we can only get to a better life. To kill or to die. Sometimes that's what it is all about."

My friend was quiet. He said absolutely nothing, something really unusual for him. That's why, that very night, when we were alone, I asked him:

"What did you think about the Legionnaire?"

"That guy is dangerous. What he's said about death isn't a bluff. He isn't afraid of dying; he's madder than he looks, much more."

"Come on! Really?"

"Didn't you notice? When you talk to someone you must look at him carefully. You must see how people react when you bother them, when you flatter them, when they tell the truth and when they lie. You can create a battery of questions and analyse their replies and the reactions you get. It's like probing somebody until you find the place that makes him laugh, the one that makes him bleed... Once you know where they hurt, you can press to hurt them; once you know what makes them laugh, you can seek their complicity. We all have things that make us weak. People who are self-assured and hard can collapse unexpectedly too. The skill consists of quickly finding those weaknesses and knowing how to exploit them. In that game, you must also hide your cards, because you have frailties too. Like in the game of chess, there's no better way to defend yourself than to keep the enemy king constantly in check. While your adversary tries to escape from the check-mates, he can't assail your pieces. Only a few, very few, reach a high level. In that case, the game is more exciting, the victory more highly prized. Crazy people don't follow a predictable pattern, that's why I like them so much, they're always a challenge. One of the things I always do when I meet somebody is to evaluate if they are more disturbed than me."

"Am I crazier than you?" I asked, intrigued.

"No. You'll never be crazier than me. You're only hindered by your shyness. You are shy and that makes you always anxious, worried, fearful, insecure, self-conscious, irritated. What others think about you worries you; your shyness makes you worry you might look like an odd guy to others; you get irritated because people take advantage of you because you're so shy; you're angry because you're unable to reply to those selfish people how they deserve… Everything makes you live in a permanent state of instability and anger. You're only able to conquer your shyness through fury, it's the only thing that allows you to break the shackles that keep you timid but that's not the way to conquer it and later you regret it and your insecurities and anxieties return. That's all, a simple minor matter of shyness and anger, nothing serious."

I got anxious. He'd made such an accurate diagnosis that I felt ridiculous and vulnerable. Was I so transparent? Was it so noticeable? I felt the heat in my face: the blood rushed up and I was blushing terribly. What an idiot! I immediately felt annoyed, but I realised that would prove his point even more, and so I tried to calm down by looking the other way. My friend knew me well and, aware that if he looked at me everything would get worse, decided to change the subject while he turned his back on me, pretending to pick up something from the floor.

After a few seconds, when my face was recovering its normal colour, he started talking again.

"Ah, by the way, the Legionnaire is crazier than I. He's dangerous, very dangerous."

I listened for a while to see if it was one of his jokes – it was typical of him to get out of something with a joke – but he didn't add anything else. I was so surprised I completely forgot my previous anger. The Legionnaire hadn't looked especially dangerous to me. A weird guy like many others, with his ghosts and his stories, with his theories and his things. Peculiar? For sure. Dangerous? Neither more nor less than the rest, including the Tarahumara. However, my friend was very observant and used to seeing things I didn't. He was also very self-assured. So much so, it didn't bother him to admit that he felt surpassed, although it didn't happen often. What's more, it was the first time he'd ever told me something like that.

The next day, they woke up us early. The Tarahumara came by with two horses and two cowboy hats for us. My friend had some idea, but I'd never gone riding in my life. I froze up and looked at him, seeking support. He laughed.

"Only a question. Where's the break?" he said, smiling.

"Don't you know how to ride? *Pinches* Spaniards! Good for nothing!"

"A bit of respect, please, that we brought you the horses."

"What do you mean you brought them?"

"Yes. The Spanish conquistadores were the ones who brought you the horses, the mirrors, the wheel..."

"Hop on the horses and stop the nonsense," he ordered, somewhat angry.

"Wait a minute," my friend told me, taking me to one side. "I'm going to give you a bit of advice, to make it easier for you. The first thing is to introduce yourself to the horse. It's not a motorbike; it's a living and intelligent being, with a personality, capable of noticing if you are feeling secure, fearful, doubtful, if you care... Approach him slowly, with determination, from the front and with your hand extended so he can see you clearly and he has a chance to smell you. Also, that way you'll make it lower its head, and that always amounts to a degree of submission. You must always pay attention to its ears. If it stretches them and turns them back, it's scared or angry. If it does that, you must be very careful and never stand behind it. Horses kick in a straight line and that differentiates them from cows that do a sweeping lateral and back movement. When you move around a horse, always keep touching him with a hand. It

172

will feel that you're moving without losing your position, and it won't get nervous."

"You know a lot about horses, smartass."

"I had one a long time ago: a gorgeous Spanish thoroughbred. They sold it to me for a good price because it was already too old for competing. It was trained in dressage: piaffe, passage, Spanish step... A wonder."

After complying with the whole protocol of caresses, pampering, security and submission, the horse I chose – my friend allowed me to choose – seemed to get on well with me. They helped me mount and we started riding around the area.

At first, I was nervous and I tried to steer it as if it were a bike, to avoid objects. Then I realised I didn't need to do that, it could do it perfectly by itself. Then I tried the walk, trot and gallop. Everything well except for the trot. I didn't get the hang of it, I was bouncing up and down on the saddle and I hurt my back. In the meantime, my friend had cracked his horse without any problem, even though they had told us it was more nervous and rebellious than mine. He was sitting tall and confident, with his cowboy hat, as if he'd never done anything else in his whole life.

We rode for a couple of hours and I ended up exhausted. My legs hurt from squeezing them against the saddle to avoid falling off, my back hurt due to the trot, and I felt the tension all over my body. If I had to ride a long time in the days to come it'd be torture. As soon as I dismounted, I went straight to bed.

The animals, wrapped in a cloud of yellow dust that obscured the dawn sun, started arriving from very early morning. They had rounded up as many as they had been able to, as the price per head was much higher than usual. When they were all together, I was very impressed: there were many more than I had expected. It didn't look easy; we had to transport a huge herd, but I trusted the good work of those people.

The hamlet stirred up with the arrival of the cows. Usually, it looked abandoned, with the few inhabitants always hiding inside of their houses to escape the heat of the day. Now it was full of life. Between the people in the village and the ones bringing the animals, we were a group of around thirty. A general feeling of joy and joviality filled up the atmosphere of that bustling morning.

When all the animals had arrived, we hopped onto the horses and went straight to the Río Grande; they needed to drink. I was trying to stay a bit away from the cattle; I felt a measure of respect for all those animals: hundreds of legs and horns, with their tongues hanging out to ease the heat and their eyes expectant. My friend travelled by my side, although sometimes he went ahead to inspect something.

It was an impressive scene, like in the cowboy movies: on horseback, wearing our cowboy hats, we were crossing the dry plains surrounded by a huge herd. The bellows of all those cows were around us, chasing away the impressive silence of the desert and stunning our heads. We moved forward slowly under a fiery sun, accompanied by the strong smell of the animals. My nose, totally dry, hurt when I breathed. The horses were foaming at their mouths and were sweating buckets; the dust got stuck to their sweaty bodies creating a nasty yellowy paste.

I felt like a tough guy. I had progressively forged my toughness with my walks and adventures. My figure wasn't the same as when I'd arrived in Mexico. In such a short time, that soft, tender and scared student had become a rough and tough as nails male, used to exercising and to dangers. I was convinced that it was evident in my attitude, in my demeanour, in my eyes.

My friend came close to me and murmured, stealthily:

"I can't see the drugs or the weapons, but, as is the case with God, he does exist."

"What?"

"Don't you tell me you believe this is all about cows and protecting the flora, do you?"

"No, of course not," I lied, somewhat disturbed.

"We're passing something more than simple cows from one side of the border to the other, but I haven't yet found out what or how. Let me know if you see anything."

My maleness and my toughness disappeared quickly and cruelly. I hadn't thought about it, but, once my friend had opened my eyes to the possibility, I was convinced we were bringing something illegal into the United States. What made me angry was not having sensed it before. I blushed slightly; I was still naïve. My fears and my insecurities returned.

We reached the river without problems and left the cattle drinking in peace; they needed to recover and get ready for the long journey still ahead of us. We took the chance to refresh ourselves. The heat was coming down hard and it was very enjoyable to soak our heads, even if it was in those warm and contaminated waters. Contrary to what I had thought, the mythical Río Grande wasn't anything to write home about, at least at the end of August. It wasn't very deep and the water didn't cover us up; the animals waded through the river without problems. Once on the other side, already in the United States, I felt a strange sensation, thinking how easy it had been to cross such a famous border. It felt unreal to be in another country already.

More than half of the people who were coming with us didn't cross the river; they stayed in Mexico. The herd seemed calm and compact and moved slowly and at a constant pace; although the group had reduced a lot, we were enough to control it.

After a while, some United States Park Rangers came to meet us. They only talked to the Tarahumara, who showed them some papers. My friend approached them and they all talked together for a bit.

"What did they say?" I asked him when he came back.

"Nothing. They're in cahoots with these people. They also get dollars out of this. They've just played their part and have asked for some papers they didn't even study closely."

After a very long march through the desert, with a merciless sun cruelly pummelling our bodies and drying our souls to their deepest recesses, we finally arrived. Civilisation took the form of a simple but asphalted road. Next to it, there was a vast fenced area where they allowed us to leave our animals. We did it without problems, helped by the skill of the people waiting for us there. Immediately afterwards, trucks arrived there to transport the cows. Thanks to a chute they had prepared in advance, the operation was relatively easy, although it took some time. Once they were all loaded up, I thought our job had finished. I was wrong.

"You must accompany the cattle to their destination. It's only a few hours by truck."

I looked at my friend, to see if he'd say something. He only shrugged, extended his arms and looked at me with an expression between amused and resigned.

"OK, then!"

Chapter 18. The Lucky Clover

The owner of the Lucky Clover ranch was from the United States, of Irish descent. His grandfather had immigrated to America in search of fortune and he'd managed to find it. Despite that, he always felt homesick for his Irish home, a poor and green Ireland, famished and enigmatic, always wrapped in a fog. A land he ended up hating due to the constant hunger and fear of his childhood; but, once he abandoned it, he remembered it with nostalgia. When he arrived at the United States, poor as a rat, he could only take with him a suitcase with a couple of changes of clothes and a Holy Bible. Inside the Bible, there was a four-leaf clover his mother had given him. The shamrock has been the symbol of Ireland since Saint Patrick used it to explain the mystery of the Holy Trinity to the Irish, and his mother gave it to him to remind him of his origins and his religion, but also to bring him luck. Perhaps it was the clover, perhaps not, the thing is that he managed to prosper thanks to hard work, perseverance and, of course, a little luck. He made lot of money and his wealth increased when he got married to a rich Texan girl. Once married, as often happens, he moved to live in his wife's homeland. There he quickly got to control the family business and accumulated large amounts of cattle and land. However, the good Irishman still missed the green prairies from his home and he built his ranch in such a way that it reminded him of his origins. He wished to bring a little bit of Ireland to Texas, a somewhat bizarre and expensive idea, although understandable and affordable for somebody of such means. He surrounded his ranch with a large green prairie and, he wouldn't have it any other way, planted tonnes of clover. When he managed to get hold of some four-leaf ones, he invested vast amounts of money in selecting them and he managed to reproduce that genetic anomaly. He achieved a much higher proportion of them than anywhere else in the world. The clover brought him luck, and that's how he lived rich and happy during his intense and full life.

When the old Irishman died, everything went to his son. The son inherited his father's good intuition to make money, and the fortune and the clovers continued to keep company with the family. Years later, the Irishman's grandson inherited the famous Lucky Clover, also known as the Four-Leaf Clover for evident reasons. Of course, he kept the clover prairie, not only because it was the ranch and his own family's hallmark, but because he also believed clover was the reason for his business success. It appears that the strict honesty of the religious Irish grandfather got diluted over time and that was how the grandson, whom we met, got involved in the shady business we were busy with at the time.

Our cattle-trucks reached a spectacular ranch. At the entry, we were welcomed by a huge sign with a four-leaf clover painted on it; Lucky Clover was written right underneath in huge green letters. The ranch was enclosed by a pretty wooden fence. Inside the fence, there was a huge field full of clover. They must have used an incredible amount of water to keep it so green, and water for sure wouldn't be cheap in such an arid zone. At one of the ends of the ranch stood the zone where we unloaded the animals: it consisted of a fenced wide area of dried-up soil next to the ranch. Seen from the air, the two fenced areas had the shape of a number eight, with both enclosures separated only by a short stretch of the palisade.

The ranch workers took care of watering the animals. The Tarahumara, my friend and I walked to the green ranch. The rest would have dinner and sleep in the servants' house, next to the dusty animal enclosure.

When we entered the main building, we were welcomed by one of the servants. He took us to our rooms on the first floor and suggested we take a bath before dinner. He said it in a way that made it look like he didn't trust our personal hygiene much. As if we weren't going to clean up after that journey! I'd been dreaming of having a good shower for several days, so in my case, I thought it was an unnecessary comment. He also insisted – to the point of appearing impertinent – on the exact time when we should be ready for dinner. The truth is I didn't like him very much: without knowing each other at all, he'd already called us filthy and unpunctual.

"It's late and we don't have much time," my friend said, seriously and firmly. "Only a final question:

should we wash with soap or will it be sufficient to use abundant water?"

The servant was about to reply, but I couldn't help my laughter and he left, offended.

I entered the room I'd been assigned. Over the door, there was a huge pair of horns. Two old photos, in black and white, were the only decoration on the walls. In one of them there was a hunter with a dead bear at his feet; in the other one, the same person appeared with his foot resting on some kind of wild goat. The furniture was sparse but seemed of good quality. Over the Mexican blanket that covered the bed, they'd left pressed and clean clothes ready for me. When I opened the door that connected with a small and shiny bathroom, I nearly started jumping for joy.

I had a good shower, with the water quite cold, which allowed me to get rid of the heat and the dust accumulated. I only became aware of the strong smell of my clothes once I was clean. It was a ripe mixture of sweat and the smell of cow, horse and soil. I left my dirty clothes on the floor, piled up in one of the corners of the bathroom – I couldn't find a better place – and I got dressed in the clothes provided. The shirt was too big; therefore I rolled the sleeves up to my arms' length. Instead of a standard tie, I had a bolo tie, like the rodeo cowboys. With the denim trousers, they'd guessed right, and they fitted me quite well. Once dressed-up I contemplated myself in the mirror; I looked quite funny.

Someone knocked at my door and I got worried, but it was only my friend. When he saw me dressed like that, he laughed at me and I felt a little bit ashamed. His dress was quite interesting too and I ended up smiling also.

We were the first ones to go down for dinner; the Tarahumara took a long time. He had also had a shower; it was evident because his long black hair was still wet. Unfortunately, afterwards, he'd donned his dirty clothes again. The filthy man had not accepted the clothes they had lent us! I began to wonder about the meaning of the insinuations they'd made about us before…

Then, our host arrived.

The dinner was sumptuous. We drank Californian wine and ate copious amounts. I had imagined we'd be joined by more people, but it was only the four of us: the Tarahumara, the ranch owner, my friend and I. I wasn't sure which language we were going to use and, with my limited knowledge of English, I was a bit worried, but I was lucky.

"What language do you want to speak?" Mister Gleeson asked, in a posh Spanish accent. "Everybody who works here is from Mexico. In mid-nineteenth century the USA declared war on Mexico and took away half of its territory, all these Southern lands. Mexico hasn't bothered shooting a single bullet to recover them; it has simply gone ahead with what they call the Silent Invasion. They've immigrated en masse for years and they've established themselves here. Now, there are so many Mexican people in the south of the United States that one could say they've reconquered it. Spanish is spoken, Mexican food is eaten, we follow Mexican customs, etc. This is more Mexican than tequila."

It was a very pleasant dinner. The owner of the Lucky Clover told us about the ranch and his family, especially about his famous Irish grandfather; about the hunting and the animals of the area. He told us many anecdotes and we didn't have to talk about any bothersome subjects. My friend said the word pumpernickel four times, which meant he won a competition where he had no rival. When we finished dinner, I was exhausted and a little drunk. I went to bed and didn't wake up until I heard the screams…

What a mess was waiting for us next morning!

Chapter 19. The Traps

I'd been locked up at home since Bad Quique's death. At first because of the fever; later, because my parents didn't allow me to go out. Although I was fully recovered, they worried I might relapse.

I got up and hungrily ate breakfast. I pretended to be happier than I was to ensure they would finally let me go out. I needed to know what had happened or I'd go mad. My friend's visit hadn't been much help, rather the opposite.

To my dismay, they didn't let me go out early, but I was lucky and my friend came to collect me. He arrived around midday, happy, whistling. He brought his fishing net and diving goggles.

"Let's go to the beach to fish crabs, that way we can talk and you'll be entertained," he ordered me.

"They won't let me do that. They've been a pain since I got ill. They worry I might relapse."

"Don't worry. I'll sort it out."

I nodded and straight away I started putting my trunks on. I had no doubt he'd be successful.

As soon as we left the house, on our way to the beach, I asked him, bluntly:

"Anything new? Any news about Bad Quique? Tell me everything you know."

"There's nothing new: they haven't found the body, the police haven't talked to anybody yet and the Baddies have apparently disappeared. Other than what I told you about the conversation of those old gossips, I haven't heard anything else. Let's go crab fishing; it will do us good to forget all about that for a while. And, we haven't checked the traps for several days; they must be bursting with crabs."

I thought he was right: the beach and a bit of exercise would be good for me, and the cold water swim would help me forget the anxieties and fears that tormented me. What better way to keep myself amused than collecting the crabs in the traps? I loved it so!

At first, I thought what I was seeing was some sort of net. After all, the same had happened to me when I had checked Dark Shadow's traps. It was an area crowded with algae, and that made it difficult to see clearly what was there. I was sure it wasn't one of our traps; it looked too big for that. Whatever it was, it was quite deep, and I had to breathe in a lot of air for the dive. As I got closer, the image became clearer. My eyes, used to trying to make out identifiable shapes, knew how to distinguish a crab from an alga, but not something unexpected. As I approached, I thought it wasn't a net; it was a dead fish. Then I saw some crabs and I dove even deeper to catch them. I focused on them and didn't see the whole image any longer. There was a huge crab and I swam towards it. When I stretched my hand to grab it, the algae moved. I focused farther from the crab and managed to see what was at the bottom. The bulge I had seen at the start was neither a trap nor a big fish. It was a drowned man! I saw a whitish face, swollen and torn, with empty eye sockets. A drowned man! I got so scared I swallowed up water and had to go back to the surface quickly. The retching for having swallowed those rotten waters, together with the horrible image I had seen, made me vomit. I was trying to keep afloat, but it wasn't easy. I was desperately moving my arms and legs to avoid sinking, but I was drowning amidst the water and my vomit.

My friend came quickly to help me and took me to the shore. I spat in between gasps and I coughed in my attempt at getting some air into my lungs. It took me a few minutes to recover; I was exhausted, traumatised, disgusted and sick. Only then was I able to tell him, still trembling, what I had seen. The horrible image that has never left my mind since.

He didn't ask me anything, only blurted out the terrible and killer line I didn't want to hear.

"It's Bad Quique."

I lost my colour. What he had said had to be true. Who else could it be? However, to avoid facing it, I tried to lie to myself.

"I couldn't see him well; it could be any person who's drowned."

"But what on earth are you saying? If it was somebody from here, we'd be aware of his disappearance. There's only one person missing: Bad Quique. He drowned and a few days later the body of somebody drowned appears. What else do you need? Anyway, don't worry. I'll dive and check if it is him," my friend said.

"No, please. Don't do it."

He didn't even listen to me. He left me trembling on the shore and went. I contemplated him, horrified. Luckily, he didn't take long to come back.

"It's Bad Quique. Yes, sir."

"Is he?"

"Yes, he is. He's not looking too good, but the trunks are the same. And, who else could it be? You're lying to yourself because you don't want it to be him, but he is. I imagine it's some kind of irony that it is us who've found him. A twist of fate; it seems God has a peculiar sense of humour."

"And what do we do now?" I asked, horrified.

"We go home. Do you have any better ideas?"

"Shouldn't we report it to the Guardia Civil?"

"No. It's better not to say anything; otherwise, they'll start asking questions about the traps and the dead man. They always suspect the first people who find the body."

"His mother should know it. It doesn't seem right."

"Don't worry about that; the tide will drag him out soon. Tomorrow he'll appear on the beach."

My friend was mistaken; he appeared on the beach that afternoon.

Once the Guardia Civil took over the case, a big secrecy surrounded the investigation. Nobody in the village knew anything, it was all conjectures. I was petrified; I could hardly eat; I couldn't sleep; I was a zombie. And on top of that, I had to pretend in front of my parents so they wouldn't suspect anything. It was torture. I wanted to forget the whole thing, to escape and I wanted it to disappear forever, but there it was and I couldn't help it. Once we'd reached that point, I needed to know how the investigation was progressing: when you know you're guilty and you can't escape, the worst thing is the lack of news. I didn't know anything, I was going mad.

My friend arranged to meet me at the beach. I turned up, anxious and overwhelmed.

"What has happened with Bad Quique?"

"As you well know, he's been found drowned."

"Yeah, thanks, fucker. Tell me something I don't know!"

"There isn't much else to know. The police have been talking to the Baddies and to some people from the village. They asked the father of a neighbour if he'd seen anything strange recently. It wasn't for any specific reason, only because he gets up very early and goes to the harbour every morning."

"They must have discovered something…"

"They don't know anything. They don't have anything. We don't know what version the Baddies have given the Guardia Civil, but I'm sure they haven't mentioned us, otherwise they would have interrogated us already…"

"Nothing else?"

"My mother met Bad Quique's mother in church yesterday. She hasn't been able to bury her son yet because the coroners are still investigating it. She was crying, calm and resigned. She told my mother, who hasn't stopped thinking about it, that she felt bad for losing him, but she also felt liberated. I imagine Bad Quique caused her more than a few troubles… I don't know… Perhaps it's the best thing for her."

"Have you tried to talk to the Baddies?" I asked, anxiously.

"No," he concluded, sharply. "Best not to mention it. Let's keep quiet. We'll try to obtain information from our families and the people from the village. Although everybody is pretending they don't want to talk about it, there is no other subject of conversation around."

"They'll ask us eventually," I said, scared.

"Let's make a pact. I don't want you to be frightened when somebody asks you because you're right," he said, looking at me, "the questions will come sooner or later, that's for sure. Always remember that Bad Quique made our lives a misery, hence no remorse for that bastard."

"Don't be a brute; he's dead."

"Tact is something I killed and raped when I was only ten years old. Don't be a pushover. Bad Quique's death changes nothing. He was a bastard before; he's a dead bastard now. We can add other adjectives, but I won't remove bastard. Or are we going to start now saying he was a wonderful person, a friend of his friends, good and generous? Remember that I could be dead because of him. What's more, logic dictates I should be dead and he alive; he's stronger and older than me. I don't owe him anything, not even a miserly explanation, not a moment's sorrow, not the tiniest guilt feeling… I don't forget you could also be dead; you were supposed to jump next. And, the village is now a better, prettier and more peaceful place. That swine isn't there any longer making our lives miserable and the Baddies have all but disappeared; they're nothing without their leader."

I shut up. He was right.

"Well, let's get on with it. We must make a pact of silence. OK? Pact!"

He solemnly approached me, looking me in the eyes and shaking my hand vigorously.

"Pact," I repeated.

We sealed our pact that way. Neither of us would say anything. I knew he'd never talk and I wouldn't either.

That afternoon was particularly active. We played football with energy, we ran faster, we swam with more rage and we laughed out louder. It was a celebration of our freedom. We were free; we had defeated Bad Quique and death. We were alive and conscious of it. We wanted to enjoy it, and we stayed lying down on the beach, the waves practically disappeared; only the sun was left, red and reflected on the sea. We smoked our final cigarette, which tasted glorious, before returning home, happy.

Nothing indicated the anxieties would return…

The days went by without anything important happening. We didn't get any noteworthy news about Bad Quique, despite paying attention to anything the town's people said about it.

Although it didn't add anything new, my heart missed a beat when my father showed us the article in the newspaper. It appeared in the section of accidents and crimes, next to a picture of a beach that had nothing to do with the village. The story, short and concise, said he'd drowned and little else. It's true that it linked the village with illegal drugs.

'…Dies drowned, in strange circumstances, E. S. T., a local youth, eighteen years old… Causes unknown… No scenarios are ruled out… The Guardia Civil is investigating the strange death… It could be related to drugs, something usual in these coastal villages, where the traffic of illegal substances has exponentially increased in the last few years…'

One thing was clear; the reporter who'd written it wouldn't win the Pulitzer.

The village bells tolled the death knell. After the delays due to the investigation, finally, the day of the burial had arrived.

Bad Quique wasn't exactly well liked, but his mother was and the whole village wanted to show her their support. My parents insisted on going. The Baddies were there, but they didn't dare get too close to Reme, I don't know if due to respect or fear. She was dressed in black, surrounded by several elderly women also wearing rigorous mourning; one of them was holding on to her arm. Although she was quite young, that day she seemed to have grown older suddenly: stooped and hesitant, she could hardly walk.

The journey to the cemetery felt endless. We walked slowly up the slope that climbed to the edge of the cliffs but it felt as if we didn't move, as if we'd never get there. We were all silent, looking down, walking tiredly. It was as if we'd all lost our energies at once and we were making a supreme and exhausting effort. The atmosphere was charged; the clouds covered the sky, the fog advanced slowly down the mountain like a wild beast crawling sinuously towards its prey. Spellbound by the penetrating breath of the forest, with its thick eucalyptus smell, we looked like zombies. It started to drizzle; the fine and soft rain fell, slow and constant, monotonous and persistent. We were all carrying something that weighed us down enormously: the youths, the drenched clothes; for the adults, the heavy umbrellas felt as if they were made of solid lead. The effort made us all breathe through our mouths, gasping. The dense fog was suffocating us. Reme cried unhurriedly, drops of water running down the tips of the bangs of her soaked and greasy hair. Somebody had tried to offer her an umbrella but she had rejected it with a slight movement of her hand. She looked absent, lost, empty of anything beyond concentrating on her next step. The only will she had left was to reach the cemetery.

Finally, we arrived, soaked, to that isolated place. The cemetery was as lugubrious as the rarefied atmosphere surrounding us. Only the small plants that grew in the cracks and on top of its walls brought some life to that sad image. While the priest talked, the mother's moans increased. I gazed at the sea. Rough and grey, it looked as if it was sharing the feelings of those present. The view was impressive. From the little cemetery, the dead could contemplate the sea until eternity or from it. When the priest finished, it stopped raining and we all left quickly. We went down much faster than we'd gone up, and more fluidly. I don't know if it was the joy of having already swallowed the bitter pill or the happiness of being still alive, but the atmosphere had undoubtedly changed. I walked ahead of my parents on the way down. I was a bit apart from the rest when Pirulo, the village madman, joined me. I didn't see him arrive, he approached me from behind; I hadn't even noticed his presence at the burial. He put his hand on my shoulder and whispered:

"I saw you at the Rock of the Missing."

I gave such a jump that I nearly fell down. My parents saw us and came quickly.

"Leave my boy alone. This is not the time!" my father said, curtly.

Pirulo mumbled something and left, singing:

"They all laugh,

All those liars,

All who live

Find death."

"Did that madman scare you?" my father asked me.

"You're very pale. Are you feeling well?" my mother added, worried.

"Don't worry about it, he just caught me by surprise," I protested, my pulse still accelerated.

It started raining again, this time hard, angrily. We did the only thing one could do in such circumstances: go home.

I showered and went to bed early. I was tired, frozen and frightened to death. Everything kept going round in my head until the early hours. The questions were again rushing in my head. What did Pirulo know? Was he going to betray us? Would everybody end up knowing the truth? A new wave of fear flooded my body. When the fear was receding slightly, it would start again. Bloody Bad Quique was coming back from his grave; he reincarnated himself to carry on tormenting us. It was torture, a nightmare turned reality.

Chapter 20. Man Hunters

After the sumptuous dinner at the Lucky Clover, I had gone to bed and slept like a log. I was so tired I didn't wake up the whole night. The dawn arrived and I was still pleasantly asleep. I was dreaming. In my dream, I was diving in a paradisiacal beach, surrounded by millions of gold fishes in a huge coral reef. Everything was calm; the fishes looked at me without any fear, as if I were one of them. Then, the screams started and all the fishes got scared. I woke up startled.

I peered through the window and saw a funny image: the cows grazing peacefully in the green prairie of the ranch and the employees running after them, fighting, unsuccessfully, to get the animals out of there. Mister Gleeson ranted impotently. He didn't want to use the horses because their hoofs would ruin the clover field for sure, but in the end, there was no other option. It was too late: the prairie now wore a battered look.

It seems that, for some reason, when we arrived they had only watered the animals but did not feed them. Compelled by their hunger, the poor cows managed to bring down the palisade trying to reach the hankered-after clover in the early hours.

The owner was distraught, furious. He went to check the palisade and came back stomping in large strides. He was shouting in English and I was no longer able to understand what he was saying. He was like a madman. One of his men came to the house and told us it would be best if we left; they didn't need us any longer and we had to go back to Mexico. We followed his advice and were ready in a few minutes. We had no other possessions than what we were wearing and that wasn't even ours, therefore we had nothing to gather and no suitcases to pack.

We left, driving towards the South in an old pickup truck. In front, in the cabin, was the Tarahumara with the Legionnaire and another person; in the back, in the cargo bed, rode my friend and I. The rest of the people weren't coming back with us. Where did they go? Better not to ask, just in case.

My friend seemed very happy. I was also feeling hopeful about returning to Mexico; I was embracing the possibility that the whole adventure would end up well. Even with that, the trip felt quite long. I didn't cope well with the enormous heat of those lands. On top of the metallic truck, with the sun hitting hard, I was getting scorched. The breeze created by the movement of the vehicle was dry and burning, to the point that it felt more like a punishment than a help. The hat did help, though, but not enough. Although we used some blankets we found in the bed to avoid lying directly over the hard and hot metal, the jolting was very uncomfortable. We were loose, not held by anything, in that metal box; if the driver breaked suddenly we'd surely end up dead.

After several endless hours, we reached the place where we had loaded the cows on the way out. My friend pointed out that there was nothing left of the structure that had been there before; both the enclosure and the chute to load the animals in the trucks had disappeared. He was right; they'd dismantled the whole lot. There was no trace of any of it left.

There, we found a guy waiting for us with five horses and a mule carrying big parcels. I assumed they contained food and blankets, but who knows… I was getting used to mistrusting everything and everybody. We had to ride across the desert once again to go back to Maderas del Carmen. My horse was the same one as the previous time and I was happy; I had grown fond of the animal already. It also recognised me.

"Now that everything has gone well, can you tell us the truth? It wasn't only a matter of cattle, was it?" my friend asked.

"No," the Tarahumara replied, smiling. "Of course there was something else, there's always something else. Clever boy the Spanish *pinche*!"

"Was it drugs?"

The Tarahumara seemed surprised.

"How can you know? Did somebody talk too much?" he asked, turning towards the Legionnaire.

"Do you think I'm an idiot?" replied the Legionnaire, his eyes showing such contempt and hatred that the Tarahumara got frightened.

"Well." The Tarahumara hesitated. "What does it matter? Now I can tell you, there's no danger: it was cocaine. The plan was easy: the animals carried the drugs inside. Why use people as mules when we can use animals? A cow is capable of carrying plastic balls, full of drugs, in amounts unthinkable for human beings. And, there's no device that can detect the drugs inside of those animals. Conventional x-ray machines aren't big enough for those animals. It was only a matter of making them eat them and in less than twenty-four hours they'd be in the United States. Impossible to detect, perfect business.

"That's why they didn't feed them when we arrived, isn't it? I thought that was strange."

"True. Usually, the animals aren't able to expel the balls when they shit; they have to be cut up to extract them. Even with that, we were worried some might come out. To keep the animals fasting seemed the safest option, but nothing will happen just because they've eaten a few bloody clovers. In the worst-case scenario, we'd lose a few balls with drugs. We've put so many in that they'll become rich anyway… The gringo will be able to replant his green prairie. By now, the animals will be on their way to the abattoir, if they aren't there already. We have paid the workers off: when they clean the insides and extract the stomach, they'll remove the drugs. Nobody will know anything; it's all well planned."

"Very clever," my friend admitted. "A very good plan."

We'd been riding for half an hour when we found some guys armed with rifles waiting for us. I noticed the Tarahumara tensed up.

"This wasn't in the script," my friend whispered. "Danger: these ones haven't been paid off."

The guys blocked our way. There were four horsemen. They formed a tight line before us. Their rifles were intimidating because, although they were pointing up, they were out of their holsters. I remembered the cowboy movies from my childhood, those horsemen duelling under the sun. The problem was that it wasn't a movie. It was real life and I didn't have John Wayne by my side.

"They are wetback hunters. Gringos sonsofbitches," muttered the Legionnaire right before spitting on the floor, leaning to one side of his horse.

The Legionnaire, my friend and I remained a few steps behind. The Tarahumara and the other Mexican who was accompanying us moved forward to talk to them. They spoke in Spanish. I heard them say we were scientists, that we were part of a team of international researchers. They were getting their paperwork out to prove their words when, without any warning, the gringos started shooting point blank. They weren't worried about missing; it seemed impossible to miss a shot.

The Tarahumara and the other Mexican were between them and us. They had no time to do anything. They were our unwitting shield and received all the shots. They covered us sufficiently to prevent them from hitting us with their first shots, at the cost of their own lives.

My friend made his horse rear up in front of me to cover me. My ride got scared and as I wasn't prepared, I fell to the floor. The Legionnaire dismounted at full-speed and, as he did, he produced a tiny machine-gun. To this day, I have no idea where it came from. He shot a burst of bullets at point-blank range that blew to bits horses, riders and everything in front of us. When he stopped shooting, all the animals and the gringos were dead or seriously wounded. He replaced the empty magazine and approached the ones alive still. With a terrifying sangfroid, he killed them off, one by one, without making any distinctions, men and horses. He didn't follow any special hierarchy, as they appeared in front of him he shot at them. When he'd finished killing them all, he turned around and came towards us. He didn't want to leave any witnesses of that massacre.

I was still on the floor, recovering from the knock I'd suffered. Once again, my friend saw the danger coming and got in first. He dismounted and came to my side.

"Legion, come to me! When they hear Legion, come to me, wherever it may be, they will all come, and whatever the reason, they'll defend the Legionnaire asking for help [Legion's Creed]."

The Legionnaire was dumbstruck. He hesitated. He'd come straight for us and was going to get rid of us. My friend's sentence had thrown him off. He put the gun down and started to walk in circles.

"You aren't a Legionnaire; I don't have to respect your life," he said, aiming at us again.

My friend remained by my side. Firm and determined. He talked in a very loud and hard voice, like a military man.

"I am a Legionnaire knight. Gran Capitán Regiment, Melilla. I was a Legionnaire and, therefore, I'll remain one all my life. I am asking for your protection, as a comrade Legionnaire; I'm also asking for it for my friend, as a protégé and friend of a Legionnaire."

"You're lying. Why didn't you say anything before? If you were a Legionnaire you would have told me."

"How would I know the Legion's Creed if I weren't a Legionnaire?"

The Legionnaire carried on walking in circles. A big debate seemed to be taking place inside of him. At some points, he would aim his gun at us; at others he would shake his head and lower the weapon.

"Even with that, I'm not a Legionnaire; my father was the Legionnaire, not me."

"Your father was a Legionnaire. A great man that instilled worthy values in you. You have those values: the spirit of the fight, of death, of suffering and of companionship. You can't betray a Legionnaire. You can't let your father down, you must honour his memory. And, we won't let you down either. We haven't seen anything. We won't tell anything to anybody. Those gringos deserved to die."

"I'm sorry," he said, aiming at us again.

Then, my friend, very serious, started singing at full volume, while he walked directly towards him.

"When the fire was roughest

and the fight fiercest

defending the flag

the Legionnaire advanced.

Without fearing the thrust

of the exalted enemy,

he died like a brave

and rescued the ensign."

He was getting close to the Legionnaire without stopping his singing. When he was by his side, he held the barrel of the weapon in his hands and aimed it at his own heart. He stopped singing for a second and then started again, louder.

"To come to visit you…"

And then the Legionnaire joined him and both sang together.

"…my most loyal companion,

I became death's fiancé,

I embraced her in a strong bind

and her love became my flaaaaag!"

It was ridiculous to see those two madmen singing in the middle of the desert. If it wasn't because of the tiny little detail that we were surrounded by dead horses and men, it would have even been funny. Up to that point, dizzy first from the fall and later terrified in case he got rid of us, I hadn't noticed the smell. A repugnant smell, a mixture of sewer and blood enveloped us and suffused the atmosphere. My friend and the Legionnaire looked into each other's eyes for a while. Then both of them bowed their heads to the other and separated.

"We're going."

We had no horses. Mine had escaped at the beginning, and the Legionnaire's had fled also when he started shooting. The rest were simply dead; we only had the mule.

"We have some twenty kilometres to reach Río Grande and cross the border. Only then will we be safe," affirmed, the Legionnaire.

"Let's go, then," my friend replied.

"Your friend will ride the mule with all the weapons and the provisions," the Legionnaire added. "You and I will run through the desert. I want you to grab one of those rifles from the gringos and raise it above your head, and I'll do the same. We'll run like that until one of us falls down. After a while, you'll feel a terrible pain in the shoulders and your feet will hurt. Don't worry, that's good. The pain is your friend; it reminds you that you're still alive. It will irk you until you reach your goal. Let's see if you're really a Legionnaire…"

"I only ask one thing," my friend interjected.

The Legionnaire turned around, furious.

"Don't you dare…"

"I only want to be allowed to sing," interrupted my friend. "That we go singing together."

The Legionnaire seemed pleased.

"Let's go."

"I'm a brave and loyal Legionnaire…

I'm a soldier of the brave Legion..."

I felt somewhat stupid, riding the mule behind those two crazy guys. They were running through the empty and silent desert, with their rifles held high above their heads, singing at full blast. He'd achieved another one of his funny challenges... I felt embarrassed on seeing them behaving that way and also somewhat enraged because I knew I wasn't at their level. I was fully convinced they were aware of my weakness. They protected me, giving me a head-start they didn't need, although it was also true that somebody had to look after the mule... I didn't think of myself as a weakling. By that point, I was much harder than most of the people I knew, but competing with those kinds of people was beyond me. They played in another division.

We carried on moving towards the Río Grande. I felt good because I was alive and well. I had weapons within my reach and, at that point, I didn't have the slightest doubt about my capacity. If I had to shoot, I'd do it. If I had to kill, I'd do it. If I had to eat a raw rat, I wouldn't hesitate for an instant. We'd left the dead as they were, without burying them, lying in the desert like dogs. I was surprised by my own lack of reaction: I didn't care. I didn't feel any guilt or sorrow for them. That was the law of the strongest, the law of the jungle. There was no time to feel sorry; one simply had to carry on surviving. When you're under the sun at almost fifty degrees, there's no room for whingeing; you must invest that effort on surviving. I was toughening up and hardening more and more, although I wasn't sure if that was a good or a bad thing. What I was clear on was that such toughness could save my life. What would be considered insensitive in other places, here was necessary. I thought I had lived a life full of shyness, fears and anxieties, and I had gained nothing from those feelings. I felt the rage flooding my body. I'd had enough of that shite. The sun beat down relentlessly, heating up my head and filling it with crazy ideas.

My mule was falling behind. I got one of the rifles out. The other two carried on running and singing in the desert. I removed the safety. I caressed the gun and thrust my heels on the sides of the mule that started galloping at once. When I overtook them at full speed, they looked at me, astonished.

"Aaaaahhh!" I shouted like a madman.

Chapter 21. Heat and fury

They surrounded the house where we had taken refuge. They were coming to get revenge for the wetback hunters killed by the Legionnaire.

They had arrived at dusk, crossing the Río Grande and following our trail. We had crossed the border the previous day and, once in Mexico, we'd gone to the hamlet where we'd first met the Legionnaire.

We had time to see them coming and get ready; we didn't run away. The people of the hamlet didn't seem in the habit of running away from the gringos.

The man who spoke was from the US; he spoke in Spanish with a strong foreign accent.

"You're surrounded. If you give yourselves up you'll come to no harm. We only want to take you to our country to stand trial."

"What are we accused of?"

"Trafficking in drugs and killing several of our fellow countrymen."

"We don't traffic in drugs!" the Legionnaire shouted.

"And we haven't killed anybody either!" my friend added, quickly, half laughing and whispering at the same time: "If we're going to deny one thing, we might as well deny everything…"

I looked at him, resignedly. Once more, he made jokes when the tension ranked up.

On the floor, there was a true arsenal consisting of all kinds of weapons and munition. All the inhabitants of the hamlet – my friend, the Legionnaire, I and three other neighbours – were inside the same house, the one they thought was the most convenient. It was a simple single-storey dwelling with thick walls to try to protect the interior from the suffocating heat of the desert. It had four windows, one on each side, which made it easy to defend. The building was in the middle of a wide and flat area, without any hiding places; if they wanted to approach us they'd make an easy target. They hadn't chosen that house as a refuge by chance; those guys knew what they were doing. They were professionals.

"Perhaps you haven't noticed, my gringos, but you're in Mexico and here your laws have no jurisdiction. Didn't you realise you crossed the river to get here?" the Legionnaire asked.

"Perhaps you haven't noticed, my friend, but this isn't an official mission. Do you see any uniforms here? Have we read you your rights? If you pay close attention, you'll see we aren't even here. We're still on the other side of the river. Can't you see?" they replied, in the same ironic tone.

"Then you can come and get us, my bitches. We're waiting for you, bearing gifts."

And the party started.

The deafening noise of shooting broke the peace of the desert. The gringos numbered around a dozen; we were just half of that. Eighteen people shooting meant lots of weapons, lots of bullets and lots of noise. We couldn't aim well because we didn't want to lean too far out of the windows. They couldn't aim well either; the house, with its thick walls, was bearing the shooting well. After a while, we all stopped shooting. It made no sense to waste any more munition. We saw them get together to plan a way of finishing us off.

"What do we do now?" I asked.

"We'll go out to get them," the Legionnaire said, with conviction. "We could wait until they get tired and leave, but they won't tire. If they've come here it's because they are determined, but they don't know we're determined, too. If we wait, they'll find a way to kill us. And, right now they don't expect us to come out; they imagine it will be a long siege. They are twice our number, so we only need to kill two of them each. It isn't that complicated; a Mexican is worth more than two gringos. They're in a group; it's our chance."

It might sound crazy, but I didn't think it was such a bad idea. I was starting to reason in a way I'd never have thought before. If we waited it would be much worse. I chose an AK-47 and a gun from the pile of weapons on the floor. I placed the gun on my belt and held the AK-47 with both hands, and then I breathed deeply.

"One will go out the door, the rest through the windows. We'll run towards them and will shoot at them. Keep separate; don't get together, we shouldn't offer them an easier target," the Legionnaire said.

"Chicken the last one," my friend whispered.

And we all set off running.

They were still in a group, thinking of a long siege, of how to leave us with no water, of how to isolate us to make us surrender. They weren't expecting it at all.

I ran as fast as I could, moving diagonally to avoid getting in anybody's way. I didn't want to risk being shot in the back by one of my brothers-in-arms and tried to make sure they were not right behind me. I was running furiously. I wasn't shooting, I wasn't shouting, I was only running. I could hear my own breathing and my pulse beating, I heard my internal scream, a scream I had suffocated for a long time. I was fed up with everything and everybody, and if I was going to die I wanted to do it taking several people with me. I started shooting when I was close. I did it nonstop, emptying the AK-47 magazine, and then I took out the gun and shot it without thinking until I had no more bullets left. They were a couple of steps in front of me. I saw that my friend and the Legionnaire were almost there; they were farther ahead. Most of the gringos were on the floor; there were very few left still standing. Mad with rage, I gained speed and lunged at the first one I came to. The impact was so strong, that with the momentum we also knocked the one next to him. The three of us fell on the ground and I began hitting the first head I found with my weapon, one raging hit after another. When I thought he'd stopped moving, I felt how somebody was holding me from the back. I turned around but before I was able to react, two big hands got hold of my face and tried to pull my eyes out. I felt one of his fingers close to my mouth and I bit it with all my strength. Thanks to that, he stopped pressing and removed his hands. As I took my chance to hold his hands hard, I noticed his breath close to me. I threw my head back, to gather momentum, and I head-butted him with all my might. I felt the pain, but my rage was stronger than anything. I gained momentum again and hit his face, time and again, until he stopped moving. The blood streaming from my brow, instead of scaring me, drove me mad. It clouded my eyesight; it irritated me with its disgusting taste. Blood, blood and more blood. Heat and fury. I stood up to keep going and kill the rest and I saw there was nobody left standing. I picked up a rifle from the ground and I started shooting anybody who was lying down. I finished them off as the Legionnaire had done. I didn't want to leave anybody alive, I didn't want them to shoot me, I didn't want to wait until I had calmed down and realised I didn't dare to kill them off. I shot the wounded and the dead. I shot one, and another, and another, and another. The next one didn't need it, he was like a sieve; even then, I still shot him. Then the rage blinding my brain cleared for an instant and I realised: neither my friend nor the Legionnaire was standing. I turned around, quickly and desperately, looking for my friend. He was lying on the ground, immobile. He looked dead, but when I approached him I heard his voice.

"I'm wounded."

Chapter 22. Pirulo

In all the villages there is a madman, an idiot and a priest. Our little Galician village also had an idiot and a priest, but with regards to the madman it was different: instead of one, there were many, plenty. Among them, Pirulo stood out. Being noted as the maddest in a village famous for its legion of madmen is no mean feat. It turns you into a true contestant to the dubiously honourable title of the world champion of the deranged.

Pirulo was very mad, but he wasn't dangerous. He always dressed the same; it's possible those were his only clothes. A black leather jacket, skinny jeans and cowboy boots: that was his uniform. We never saw him dressed any other way. He didn't care if it was summer or winter, cold or hot. He had long black hair and sported a huge beard. He was very thin, strong and wiry like a leopard. His personal aroma was very peculiar: a mixture of eucalyptus, leather and wine. He always, always, went everywhere in his small trail motorbike, one of those they use to ride in the mountains. We used to think of him as the last Don Quixote, a knight riding on the back of his muddied motorbike. A guy who had defeated the system, who was truly free, because Pirulo feared nothing and no one.

Many stories circulated about him, about his life and his madness. Nobody knew where he lived. We never saw him in the mornings; he always turned up early in the evening or at night. He arrived and disappeared into thin air. He always had some money, for wine and to buy petrol for his eternal motorbike. He was furtive. He caught the best barnacles one can imagine, truly gigantic. He managed because he went to the most dangerous places, even on the days when there was a strong thunderstorm. Nobody dared do what he did; nobody in their right mind. There you have it.

He didn't have a boat; he climbed down the cliffs to obtain his enormous barnacles. He did it tied up to a rope, in areas he alone knew. With those kinds of tricks he made do, obtaining small sums of money every time he needed it. The Guardia Civil had caught him several times, and he had numerous unpaid fines. The trick was that it was impossible to seize somebody's goods when he doesn't have a bank account, a house, or any possessions. The motorbike wasn't registered to him either.

He was loved in the village, totally mad, but harmless. He had a fearless courage that made him climb onto the bridge handrail and walk on it wearing his boots. Why? Because he could. He lived with the freedom of the individual who fears nothing and nobody. Leaning on his motorbike, with a glass of wine in his hand, he allowed the rain to soak him while he sang, laughing out loud. He was pleasant to talk to and his conversation was surreal. He was capable of reciting poetry, howling at the moon at night – and it's not a figure of speech – or of regaling

216

you with some deep philosophical lecture; he liked to talk to people, preferably drunken people. He had moments of deep insight and reflection, but suddenly his mind fled. Took off on a strange and unexpected flight.

As I've said, he liked poetry. He would recite, in a grave and cracking voice, deep and husky, with a strong Galician accent. He would cite, randomly, Bécquer, Machado, Rosalía de Castro, Miguel Hernández, Quevedo, Manrique, Espronceda. Precisely, from one of Espronceda's poems came his favourite battle cry:

My bike *is my treasure,*

my God, my freedom,

my law, the power and the wind,

my only country, the sea.

And another one of Pirulo's favourite poems was by Machado:

I, for all my journeys

– always atop the wood

of my third class compartment –

carry little luggage.

There were different legends about his madness. It seems that his girlfriend abandoned him, although others said she had died. Then, something inside him broke forever. A button was left depressed in the self-destruct mechanism. He started drinking. He drank every morning and every night. He drank more and more and started using drugs. His episodes of drunkenness, together with the tablets, were awe-inspiring. He shouted and howled; he ran around naked. Some mornings he turned up asleep in a doorway in a puddle of his own vomit. Sometimes, having wet himself, he was left lying next to a street-lamp.

He had been a sailor, although, logically, he was no longer working. The skipper of his boat kicked him out, and the rest didn't want to hire him. That was at first, later he couldn't even dream of looking for a job. It was totally impossible. He lost everything he had. Whatever he didn't spend on alcohol and drugs, he simply lost. He lost his house, his car, his friends, his family and his mind. After a crazy night filled with alcohol and pills, his mind went on a one-way trip and there it remained. It never came back. Perhaps that was what saved his life. His brain couldn't put up with any more and switched off forever. It went into a different functioning mode that prevented his fuses from blowing up when the tension rose. He was ill for a while, nobody knew if he was in a hospital or in an asylum. Sometimes, he'd mention the tablets he was taking: Rohypnol – he called them "reinolas". When he went back to the village, he was already wearing his hair long, his new clothes and his madness was totally settled, although less abrupt and violent than before. He started reciting poetry and he became a poacher. Shortly after, he bought his motorbike…and he carried on the same. Nobody managed to bring him back to sanity. He never fitted into the system again. Little by little, the people who knew him before his madness died or forgot him and there was no longer anybody who remembered him differently. He was the only one left, and in excellent health. He was old, although he hardly had any grey hairs. He was a bit stooped, but still poaching. Although local youths usually challenged him, betting a few glasses of wine, nobody had managed to beat him at arm wrestling. He was a point of reference. He was our Statue of Liberty, our symbol, although he was also a warning and a reminder. He belonged to the collective memory of the village. He'd been the philosopher's stone for several generations and he would continue to be for a few more.

What people didn't know was what he told us in a moment's lucidity. We knew something the rest of the village didn't. Perhaps that didn't make him any greater, but it made him more human. For us, he went from being a myth to being a flesh and blood human being. Somebody who suffers becomes human.

After meeting Pirulo at Bad Quique's burial, it didn't take me long to go find my friend and tell him what he'd told me. I was very frightened; Pirulo had seen us and he could snitch on us. The last thing we needed was to be caught now... Fuck! The perfect plan was leaking all over, like a poorly caulked boat.

My friend, as usual, displayed his character. He made me see what I'd been refusing to see due to my fear.

"Well, well. Let's see... Let's keep calm. Let me see if I understood correctly: what worries us is that Pirulo, the maddest of the mad, might go to the Guardia Civil and tell the tale? Of course, of course, I'm sure at the police station they'll greet him with a wave because they're so very fond of him. I'd give three months' pay to see him there! It could be the funniest and most surreal thing I've ever seen. Pirulo, the best at catching barnacles illegally, going voluntarily to the police station! Do you think he'd recite his poems to them? Would he invite them to wine and seafood?"

"Don't be an asshole. He might tell somebody and that person could go to the Guardia Civil."

"Of coooourse!" my friend replied. "Someone from the village turns up to report it, saying: 'Hello, good morning, Pirulo told me the other day that he'd seen...' The Authorities interrupt him straight away: 'Sorry, who did Pirulo see? A flying dog? Don't worry; we'll locate twenty of our best men to follow that line of investigation. We won't spare resources or people.' Whatever Pirulo says is sacred. Well, of course!" he screamed, falling about with laughter.

I couldn't help laughing too. He was absolutely right. I was becoming paranoid.

Then, he started imitating Pirulo, who had a very peculiar way of talking and expressing himself.

"I saaaaw them, Your Honour. They were theeeere. They are lyiiiing, Your Honour... They told me... I was flying over them, in the land of the Green Beings. The Green Beings are good and look after us. I'm the king of the Green Beings, Your Hooooonour. Two come in and one goes out, Your Hoooooonour. Two come out and one goes in. Many are the called but few the chosen ones, Your Hooooonour.

"Is my bike my treasure,
my God my freedom,

my law, the power and the wind,

my only country, the sea."

I was laughing my head off. He was pitch-perfect. He really did the perfect impression of him. Not only of what he said but how he said it, the gestures he used. It was an Oscar-worthy performance!

"I have an idea," he suggested. "Let's go and have a barbecue on the beach and we invite Pirulo. I'm sure he'll agree. That way we can talk to him and extract all the information we can. I'm sure we'll learn something. He's a character worthy of study. He might even tell us where to get the best barnacles!"

It took us a couple of days to organise the barbecue. We had to ask for permission at home, we had to buy the food and the drinks and hope Pirulo would come by. That last part was the most difficult one because Pirulo had the gift of appearing and disappearing out of nowhere. Nobody ever knew exactly where he was until he turned up. We didn't even know where he slept. He simply turned up whenever he felt like it. It wasn't possible to go looking for him; he was always the one to find you.

"Don't worry; we'll have a barbecue. If he doesn't turn up, we'll have to repeat it another day. What a bleeping shame!" my friend joked.

The night of the barbecue arrived. The beach and the village were empty at that time of the night; it was a weekday. A big fire was burning in front of us. My friend had taken care of it – he always did – he was fascinated by fire. He looked at it for a long time, mesmerised, devotedly, without blinking. He always

221

ended up with his eyes red due to the smoke, his face full of grime and smelling of burned wood. He didn't mind, he was the master of fire, the custodian of the process, the one responsible for the flames. He contemplated how the fire grew and waned. It grew on lighting some newspapers; it waned on adding big logs and grew again when those caught fire. In the end, it left embers of a fascinating red colour.

When the embers were ready, we started roasting the chorizos. While we waited, we ate crisps and drank cheap wine from a carton. We hadn't prepared a *calimocho*, against our habits, in deference to Pirulo. He didn't like mixing his drinks; he preferred straight wine. To mix it with other things was to slight any wine, even that one. Then I thought we should have brought something to mix it with in case Pirulo finally didn't turn up... But he did.

We first heard his motorbike; then he arrived walking in between the bushes of the beach. Very like him, he smelled the wine and joined the meeting. It was exactly what we had expected. They used to say that the overdose of pills had given him superpowers and that, like the vultures with the carrion, he was able to smell the wine at a distance of many miles. Truth or myth, the fact is he turned up where we were waiting for him. He brought an empty glass. Without asking, as he normally did, he sat close by, without getting too close. We invited him to come closer and he sat between us. When we passed him the wine carton, he filled up his glass to the brim. We also offered him food, but he didn't want any of that. He drank calmly, in little and spaced out gulps. I was quiet, expectant; my friend intervened.

"I want to be the crying farmer

who looks after the soil and fertilises…"

A few instants went by. Nobody said anything. Pirulo seemed lost in thought until he started talking too.

"… a soul's companion, so early."

"I'll donate your heart for food," my friend continued. *"So much pain clusters on my side…"*

"…that even my breath hurts," Pirulo replied.

A tear dropped from Pirulo's right eye. A fat tear rolled slowly down his face until it disappeared in his beard. It came naturally; he didn't change his expression at all: he didn't look sad or as if about to cry. It simply came out of the corner of his eye and ran down his cheek. He swallowed and his big Adam's apple moved up and down as if it had a life of its own. Then he started reciting, continuously repeating.

"I don't forgive the enamoured death,

I don't forgive the discourteous life,

I don't forgive the land or the nothingness."

We'd never seen him like that. He was a madman, yes, but a happy madman. He sang; he delivered his mystical speeches, his surreal madness, but he didn't cry; he wasn't sad. We'd never seen him cry. He carried on repeating his litany for a while, progressively softer, until it became a soft whisper quietened by the crackle of the fire.

"I don't forgive the enamoured death,

I don't forgive the discourteous life,

I don't forgive the land or the nothingness."

When we could hardly hear him, my friend started to recite again in a very nice and conciliatory tone of voice, a soft tone that transmitted trust and affection.

"In the name of the winged souls of the roses

of the almond tree of cream, I call for you,

for we have many things to talk about,

my soul companion, my friend."

While he recited the last two verses, he slowly rested his hand on Pirulo's shoulder. Then, he gently removed it and there was silence again. I was impatiently waiting for Pirulo's next reaction, but he seemed to have gone dumb. My friend talked again.

"I know well what it feels like to lose somebody you love. The days pass by and you think you should forget that person, but you don't. Every day, when you wake up, he's there. Every night, when you go bed, he goes to bed with you. The time goes by and the pain continues. People tell you you'll overcome it, but you don't, so there must be something wrong with you. Or are they the weird ones? Why should you forget?"

A brief silence followed.

"I'll tell you something I've never told anybody before," my friend continued. "I've always kept it private, but I think the time has come to share it. You must swear that it won't go anywhere, that it will remain between us."

I swore and Pirulo nodded slightly, imperceptibly moving his head.

"I killed my youngest brother," my friend curtly said.

Chapter 23. Until the End

We had been shooting until falling exhausted in that desert border hamlet. By the end of the massacre, only three of us were left alive: my friend, the Legionnaire and me. That was how the anger pent-up in that atmosphere of asphyxiating heat had ended up.

Of the three, I was in the best shape. I had a cut on my brow and scratches around my eyes, nothing serious. The Legionnaire was limping; he'd got hit by a bullet in the leg. My friend had been shot in the stomach. We needed a doctor urgently.

The Legionnaire applied a tourniquet to his own leg using a piece of rope pulled very tight and he stopped bleeding. I took care of my friend's wound. It was right in the middle of his stomach. I placed a rolled-up blanket around his torso to reduce the bleeding, but it didn't achieve much. Although he was very seriously injured, he managed to mount the mule. We didn't have any other option and we left straight away; we couldn't waste any time. If we stayed there, incommunicado, they would both die. We had to find a doctor and the nearest one was very far away.

I don't know how they lived through it, but they did. We reached a road and there a pickup stopped for us. We climbed onto the bed. They were lying on the floor and I was by their side. The journey felt eternal; it was horrible and anguishing to witness my friend's suffering. I thought he'd die before we got there.

When we finally arrived in the doctor's surgery, the hope that my friend might be saved, vanished. Neither the hovel looked like a surgery, nor did that man look like a doctor. As soon as he saw my friend's wound, he shook his head.

"Nothing doing. I have neither the supplies nor the knowledge to deal with it; there are no hospitals or doctors in many miles in all directions. He will die. I'll try to save the other one. A bullet in the leg is something different; I'll get it out straight away. There's no time to waste. Stay in that room while I operate."

Tact wasn't one of his strengths. I stayed with my friend, who had heard everything, and I helped him lie on a bunk in the doctor's house. The room was small and it was very hot. My friend had a fever and was sweating. He smelled bad, a weird stink, of death. The Grim Reaper was flying over the room; one could almost sense it. I looked at him and saw his sickly expression, the shadows under his eyes, his sticky hair, his bloody bandage, his pasty skin... He was going to die and he knew it.

"You'll have to go back to Spain alone," he said, smiling. "I won't see the village again. I'll miss it."

"You're not going to die," I replied, not too convincingly.

I realised it was a stupid comment but, what did it matter?

"No. I'll live three hundred years, like Pirulo. Or perhaps I'll live less, like Dark Shadow's bull. Dark Shadow's bull..." He sighed. "I never told you how I killed it."

"Did you kill it?"

"With clover."

"With clover?"

My friend was talking with a weak thread of a voice, quickly and rushing.

"I took huge amounts of clover to it. They were wet, juicy, cool. He ate and ate until he exploded. A farmer friend of my father's, a fabulous guy from whom I learned a lot, taught me that trick. What happened is called tympanism or bloating. If a cow, in this case, a bull, eats huge amounts of clover, they generate a kind of dense foam in their stomach. That prevents them from burping; it does not let the air out. The stomach keeps growing and growing until the animal can't breathe and it dies suffocated. A hard and strong animal, weighing hundreds of pounds, shattered by the humble clover. Isn't it funny?"

Then I saw everything clearly.

"Fuck. It was you who let loose the cows in the Lucky Clover."

"Ironic, isn't it? In the end, he was right: once the clover disappeared, his luck ended. Can you imagine what must have happened a few hours after we left? A full herd of cows suffocating are a lot of cows. I'll never know; it must have been impressive. I can't imagine it would have been easy to remove the drugs with such a large number. Brave animals; they performed their duty."

"It doesn't sound like a very nice death. So many animals suffering..." I shook my head. "You're a bastard..."

"You can't abuse somebody who is dying. Don't be a beast."

He was dying and continued to take the mickey and manipulate me. I didn't know what to say.

"I want to ask you something. When I die, cut a lock of my hair and take it to the village. You must take it to the Rock of the Missing and drop it there."

"Stop fucking with me. I have no intention of ever going back to that damn rock. Stop poking at my ghosts."

"Bring me a pen, paper and two envelopes."

"What?"

"A pen, paper and two envelopes. Ask the owner of the house straight away. There isn't much time left. I must make a will. It's very important."

When I returned, my friend was sleepy, but he woke up when he heard me. I gave him the two envelopes, the sheets of paper, the pen and a book he could lean on to write.

He called me a few minutes later. He gave me the two envelopes, solemnly. They were sealed.

"Here you have two envelopes. The envelope with the number one written on it is for whenever you think you're going to die. The envelope with the number two is for when you think again you're going to die. Put them away and never lose them. They could save your life. There are no more envelopes, there are no more lives. I wish I could write seven envelopes for you as if you were a cat, but I'm only giving you two. If it happens to you again you'll have to manage without envelopes or it's game over. I give you the trick to kill the monster at the end of the first phase, and also to kill the one on the second phase. I haven't reached the third one, and now I won't, so you'll have to kill that one alone."

"You're still carrying on with your nonsense. Aren't you going to stop even now?"

"Now less than ever. I have to do several funny things and I don't have much time left. I must be quick. Swear to me you will never open them until you're about to die."

"I swear."

"Swear it on my parents."

"I swear. Listen, and what about your parents? Isn't there a letter for them?"

"Tell my mother I love her lots. Tell my brothers they've always been by my side and in the afterlife I'll look after our little brother. I join him finally; I hope I'll be able to look after him better than last time. Tell my father about the race through the desert, the shooting; tell him I was well trained. Tell him they tortured me and cut one of my fingers off but I spit it out and told them that I didn't like that one, that I wanted them to cut off another one."

"Don't make jokes. Don't be an idiot."

I felt he was going. His strength was abandoning him for good.

"Come closer. I have a final thing to tell you."

I moved closer.

"A bit closer."

I stuck to him, waiting for him to whisper something important. I was hoping he'd confide his final words to me.

He made a final effort, enough to raise his arm and slap me in the face. It was a weak slap, but so unexpected that it hurt a bit; it got me right in the eye.

"Now we're even. I owed you that punch from years ago. You don't need to feel bad any longer. Ha, ha…"

And he died laughing. He used up his final breath to punch me. Bloody idiot! Who uses up his last moments of life to punch a friend and play some kind of joke? Who finds that kind of thing funny? I looked at him and he was smiling. He'd died with a smile on his face; he couldn't take even death seriously as if he'd managed to make a joke of the most tragic moment possible. He'd taken life as a joke and death too. They used to say he laughed at birth, a truly weird thing. I don't know if it was true, but I know he was laughing when he died, something pretty weird too for those who didn't know him. An entire life dedicated to that peculiar sense of humour.

I picked up the two letters and the sheets of paper he hadn't used. When I did, I noticed something odd. Right then I realised something was missing; it was an intuition. I rummaged in the pocket of his trousers and there it was: among the pens he kept, I found the one I had just given him.

I was starting to guess his jokes. To guess is, sometimes, the beginning of reaching an understanding.
To understand is the step prior to respect and from
there to admiration, there isn't a long stretch. I found
myself smiling next to my dead friend. Then, I cried
and I laughed again. What a character.

Next day, when I was on my way to the funeral
parlour, I walked by a small fruit market. I couldn't
help myself and I bought some tomatoes. I spent my
last pesos on those tomatoes and on the burial.

Before they closed the coffin I put the pens inside
of his pocket and the tomatoes by his feet. That's how
I buried him; it couldn't have been any other way.

Chapter 24. Consequences

When I left my friend's burial there were two thugs waiting for me. They blocked my way and told me to get into a car they had parked right there, at the gates of the cemetery. They were dressed in black; they wore black sunglasses and their car was black with tinted windows. That didn't look good at all, but there was nothing I could do. When they approached me I looked around but there was nobody nearby. Nobody knew my friend; only the priest, the undertaker and I had attended his burial. The others had stayed at the cemetery and now I was at the door, totally alone.

They searched me before I entered the car. I only had my passport and my wallet on me. Inside the wallet, there was no money, only the two envelopes. Nothing of real interest to those guys.

It took us quite a while to reach our destination. Nobody talked during our journey. They were in the front seat, quiet, listening to Mexican ballads on the radio. I was in the back, quiet, thinking about what had happened to me. The long journey in the back of the car reminded me of the drives back home from my childhood summer holidays. Sad and melancholy journeys, when you knew you were leaving behind many things that would never come back. Now, I was not only leaving behind places I wouldn't visit again; but I was also leaving a friend forever.

We went straight to a ranch I recognised: the one belonging to Mr Cabeza de Vaca. As soon as we crossed the huge doors, they shut behind us.

The owner was waiting for me. He was sitting on a rocking chair, smoking on the porch. The thugs accompanied me until they had delivered me to him and then stepped back.

"Your friend died," Mr Cabeza de Vaca started. "It's a shame. In the end, the best are always the first to go…"

I thought that my friend had gone and I hadn't. If the best went first, then I was one of the… I unconsciously smiled.

"What do you find so funny, my comments or your friend's death? Now I have you with your smiles and a business that has become complicated and has caused me some losses. I don't find that funny. I've heard from some informers; now I want to hear your version. I want you to be honest with me, I beg you, otherwise, there will be pain and hurt. I'll be hurt because you'll have lied to me and you'll be hurt by the consequences of your lies."

"Why should I lie?"

He ignored my comment and carried on talking.

"As I told you the other time I saw you, I'm a vet, and therefore I'm used to dealing with animals. I have medical knowledge I know how to use with precision and, if the occasion demands it, with brutality. I'll give you some examples. There is a very effective way to castrate young bulls: it consists of tying very tight a rubber band around the testicles. The rubber band stops the irrigation, that's to say, they no longer get blood. Then the tissues progressively dry up and die. Finally, the dried up testicles drop like raisins. It's not a bad way of castrating an animal; there are worse options… I still remember my first morning castrating pigs. You grab the balls hard, to make sure the skin of the scrotum is taut, and make a cut. Then you squeeze and the testicle comes out. Once out, you pull strongly and you rip it out (you don't cut it because when you tear it out it bleeds less than when you cut it). Once torn out, you throw them at the mother and siblings, which eat them immediately. Everything without anaesthetic. You have no idea how much a hog can scream when you do that to it. When you let it free, it rubs its little bum on the ground. It's very funny; perhaps you'll do the same when we rip yours off… What do you think? The truth is I prefer the rubber band method. It's less impressive but slower. To feel how you're losing your genitals little by little causes a pain that's not only physical but also psychological. You have whole days to reflect on how they're drying up… The thing is that I can choose either way. Do you have any preference? Ah! You're no longer smiling! Better that way."

By that point, I had nothing left, not even fear. I was so fed up I didn't show all the fear he expected.

"I laughed because my friend taught me life is a joke. I've spent the last week surrounded by death. The simple fact of being alive makes me happy. Do you want me to tell you what happened? I will tell you; there's nothing to hide. Perhaps you're surprised

I survived. The Tarahumara is dead, my friend is dead, many more are dead, and I'm not dead. You might find it curious, suspicious or even unfair. I understand. Haven't you thought that sometimes it is not the strongest, the best prepared, or the best who survive? It isn't a matter of who must die. The one whose turn it is to live lives. The one whose turn it is to die dies. It was my turn to live. Are you annoyed because I've overcome what others, whom you respected more than me, haven't managed? Do you expect me to ask for forgiveness for being alive? You're wrong about me."

He stared at me for a long time.

"We pigeonhole people too quickly. First impressions are usually accurate, but sometimes we make mistakes. I was wrong about you, but that won't happen again. Bring us two chairs!"

The thugs placed two chairs facing each other. He stood up from the rocking chair and sat on one. He offered me the other to sit on. We were very close, one in front of the other.

"What's your favourite colour?"

"Blue."

"Your football team?"

"Deportivo de La Coruña."

"OK, now tell me everything that has happened since I last saw you."

I told him everything that had happened. I didn't lie or exaggerate. There was no point in doing that; I had nothing to hide. He was looking at me straight in the eyes and nodded. When I finished, he was quiet.

"Do you know what happened after you left the Lucky Clover ranch?"

"What happened?"

"I'll tell you," he said, never moving his eyes from mine. "Shortly after you left, the cows got ill. They swelled up like balloons and died. Did you know that?"

"When we left, the cattle were healthy and I haven't had a chance of hearing what happened since we left the ranch."

"You're telling the truth, but you haven't replied to my question. Did you know?"

"No. I've already told you that."

"Now you're lying."

He gestured towards one of his thugs. The brute walked up to me from behind and slapped me so hard that I fell on the floor. They helped me stand up and made me sit again. My face was burning and I felt a bit dizzy. I thought for a moment. Trying to protect a dead man made no sense, but I thought it was very mean to blame my friend for everything, even if it was true.

Another slap helped me decide: I wasn't going to tell these bastards anything.

Then, they pushed me to the floor and started beating me up. I had to bear a storm of kicks and they stomped me with their feet. I covered myself as well as I could, crouching into a ball and protecting my head with my arms. The beating didn't stop until Cabeza de Vaca talked.

"Go and get the rubber band for castration. We'll strangulate his balls and see if he starts talking, even if it is in a higher pitch."

One of the thugs went to collect the rubber bands and Cabeza de Vaca entered the house for a moment, and I was left alone with the other thug. Although I was quite beaten up I tried to think quickly. What would my friend have done in this case? I thought about telling them a story about a tomato patch... No, that wasn't the answer. Although I didn't like to have to give in, I would have to tell the truth about my friend's guilt in the matter. How far could this madman go? The castration thing didn't feel like a bluff. What would my friend have done in this situation? Would he have accused a dead man? Then I remembered: the envelopes! The bloody envelopes for when my life was in danger! They were still in my wallet. What was inside? A cheque? Money? My friend was very rich...

The thug arrived with the famous castrating rubber bands. Right when he was about to start, Cabeza de Vaca turned up.

"Can I get something out of my pocket?" I asked, quickly.

The bodyguards tensed up, but his boss calmed them with a reassuring gesture. I took out my wallet, opened it and removed one of the envelopes inside. There was only a number written on it: 1. One of the bodyguards pulled it out of my hand and gave it to Cabeza de Vaca, who had to rip it to open it. Inside the envelope, there was a piece of paper with a name:

Mr Cabeza de Vaca. The aforementioned showed it to me with an incredulous expression.

"Is the envelope for me?"

The surprise on my face must have been enormous. I didn't understand anything. How had my friend known what would happen?

"For you? Is it for you?" I asked, totally flummoxed.

When he saw my reaction, Cabeza de Vaca also looked surprised. He lowered his gaze and started reading. As he read, his expression changed completely. It went from incredulity to anger, then to laughter and curiosity. When he finished, he closed the envelope again and stared at me.

"Do you know what the letter says?"

"No," I honestly replied, feeling intrigued.

"Don't you have any idea of what it says?"

"No. My friend wrote it right before his death and gave me the sealed envelope. He made me swear I wouldn't open it. It hasn't been opened until now."

After examining the veracity of my words, he ruminated for a while. Then he spoke, very slowly.

"Your friend was an exceptional person. Much cleverer than you imagine. He knew perfectly well what would happen. It is somewhat logical to guess I'd go after you, considering what happened at the Lucky Clover... Even so, it's very funny and daring what he suggests. You're lucky to have... You're lucky to have had," he corrected himself, emphasising the tense of the verb, "a friend like that. He's saved your life."

After a brief silence, he authoritatively addressed his thugs:

"Take him with you to have a bath. He's our guest."

Chapter 25. Confessions

My friend had a younger brother who died when he was a child. It was another one of those typical stories everybody in the village knew, although nobody dared to ask about openly. It was better to speculate, imagine and suppose. I had never asked him about the matter and he'd never brought it up.

My friend looked unblinkingly into the fire and started talking.

"It all started as a game. My parents went to buy something; my older brothers went out. They left the two youngest ones alone: my brother and I. I was supposed to be looking after him. We were playing, pretending to be ninjas. In my mother's sewing box, we found some ribbons and tied them around our heads, each one a different colour. I was the black ninja and he was the white one. We were laughing and jumping from sofa to sofa. We were trying to catch each other, we were pushing each other. At a certain point, I pushed him and he fell to the floor, backwards. The sofa wasn't very high but he had a bad fall and broke his neck. A fall as we've all had thousands, but he never got up again. The rest, I remember as if it were a movie. Everything happens in slow-motion as if to better enjoy the anguish and suffering those moments caused. Trying to revive him, the arrival home of my parents, the call to the doctor, the tears, the screams of pain... I relive everything so slowly it lasts an eternity. The worse thing about it is that it was of no use. Nobody managed to bring my little brother back to me. I pushed him. It was bad luck; it wasn't my fault or my intention, but I pushed him.

"I was never able to play with him again, to tell him I loved him. I have to live with that."

We were quiet. My friend carried on looking fixedly into the fire. Although I wanted to say something, I couldn't find the words. I thought he already knew and nothing I said would make a difference to his pain. I hesitated while I thought about all that and the occasion to talk passed me by. As more time passed, my possible comments seemed more inappropriate.

And then, what we least could have expected happened: Pirulo started talking with great common sense. He talked as usual, in Spanish with a strong Galician accent, but his voice sounded deeper and huskier than usual. As if the fluidity he usually had during his moments of craziness was lost when he recovered his sanity. The words came out slowly and with difficulty, with the clumsiness of a person who hasn't talked in a long time.

"A loss tears you up inside. You feel a pain so sharp you think your heart will explode and your bowels will come out of your mouth. You want to run until you collapse dead, scream until you're dumb, but you can't manage it. You survive, and against your will, you contemplate the days going by. Nobody else is conscious of the seriousness of the loss;

life carries on, cruel and cold. The world keeps spinning and you can't allow it to go on as if nothing had happened. You're not allowed to come down, to stop spinning with planet Earth. You want to end your life, perhaps that will be the only way to stop, but the pain is so strong it prevents you from killing yourself. You delight in your own sadness; you enjoy the punishment you're suffering to redeem your guilt: being still alive. Then, you think that perhaps the only way to stop the world might be to carry on in it. To keep on suffering, so that your continued penitence helps to remind others of her death. Then you gloat even more over your misfortune. The only reason you carry on living is to take flowers to her grave. You close your eyes and remember every moment you spent together. That makes you happy and it also hurts you with an insufferable pain. You can't work; you refuse to accept that life carries on as if nothing had happened. People understand and wait for you to get over it. Everybody ends up moving on, but you don't. Time goes by, the pain should reduce but it doesn't. According to everybody else, you must face your loss. You don't manage; you aren't like that. Then you realise people are starting to wonder. According to the majority, you should get over it; it's been a long time already. They're bothered by it because they have already overcome their losses. You're a reminder that it's possible not to forget, that you might not allow it to pass. You're not thinking about that, you're only thinking about your sadness. There's no power able to mitigate it. You try painkillers and they don't work; try alcohol and it doesn't work; although you try drugs, it remains there. Your soul is lost forever in the dark jungle. You don't want to recover it, but you're aware that, even if you wanted to, you couldn't. It's lost without a way back. You didn't deserve what happened; it's not fair; life isn't fair. One day, you meet the Green Beings. They know you're broken and they don't try to fix you; they only want to test you. The challenge is very hard; you must bet your life. If you survive, they'll give you your freedom. You'd like to die trying, so you accept. Then, something unexpected happens: you pass the test. You come in and out, you're free already, although not always or forever. You have moments of freedom because you managed to pass the test, but there are moments when your pain comes back. You neither want nor can totally forget. Not even the Green Beings helped you completely. But it's true; those who see you remember her. She was so important that you, somehow, stopped the world. You've managed. Although you find some comfort in knowing there are things that matter, which one doesn't just let go, that doesn't help you be happy.

But silent, rapt, down on the knees,

As men worship God at His altar,

As I have loved you…make no mistake,

Nobody will love you like that!

The Green Beings love me because I'm their king. I'm the king of the Green Beings!"

From then on, he started to rave as much as usual. We tried to ask him some questions to redirect the conversation, but it was impossible. We didn't manage to extricate him from his madness and his poems.

When he stood up to leave, my friend got up too. He stood by his side and put his hands on the shoulders of that pitiful madman. Pirulo did the same and they stayed like that, staring at each other for several long seconds.

"Did you also hesitate?" Pirulo asked.

"Yes," replied my friend.

"Why did you choose that option?"

"I chose it to live."

"To live? To live?! You're mad! I chose it to die," Pirulo exclaimed, surprised. "Talk to Don Prudencio; he knows."

Once he'd said that, Pirulo left, singing his poems.

"Don Prudencio knows it,

Don Prudencio listens to me.

Don Prudencio guides me

Through the fire and the fight."

I was surprised. What was that about hesitating? What was that about choosing the option to live or die? I asked my friend about that conversation, but he replied he had simply played along with Pirulo to see if he could obtain any information. However, I suspected he was hiding something. I tried to insist and he put an end to the matter with one of his witticisms:

"Pirulo has dubbed me mad! Do you realise that? Pirulo! I'm the best. The King of Madness! It's as if Pelé called you a striker or Gandhi said you were a pacifist. I've achieved something spectacular. Now I'm the Emperor of the Green Beings, you must pay homage to me."

I laughed unenthusiastically. That night had left me with a bittersweet taste. Too many sad confessions, too many emotions, too many misfortunes.

Pirulo had had an unusually long moment of sanity and had told us something we didn't know, but what we were really interested in was still in the air. The fact that he'd seen us at the Rock of the Missing was a problem. What would happen if he started to have more moments of clarity? Could he end up ratting us out? After that night I started to think that Pirulo wasn't as mad as he seemed, not by a long shot.

Chapter 26. Scores to Settle

There are times when you forget to close a small window when you shut the door of your house. You leave the village, leave the county, even the country; but the window, that small window is still open and you know it. It doesn't matter how far away you are in space or time, that window irks you. Eventually, the time comes when you simply have to go back and shut the damn window. It doesn't matter how far you are, it doesn't matter how long it has been, it doesn't matter that nobody else knows. You must go back and shut it.

I was on top of the Rock of the Missing. A decade had gone by since the Bad Quique thing and everything was the same: again in the same place, about to jump. I wasn't a boy any longer; now I was a man or at least that was what I thought. I didn't feel terror, now it was only fear. Behind me was Mr Cabeza de Vaca with his two henchmen. The weather wasn't helping. It was a rainy and foggy September day. The rain fell constantly and was soaking the thugs and me. Mr Cabeza de Vaca kept dry thanks to the elegant umbrella he carried. He was dressed impeccably. I didn't know how but he didn't have a single stain on him and his hair was in perfect order, despite the speedboat journey and the climb to the Rock of the Missing.

We had fled from Mexico to Spain in Cabeza de Vaca's private jet. Everything had been quick and efficient: no waits, no hesitations, no delays. I thought that was one of the main advantages of being a millionaire: not having doubts and not having to wait. Time and comfort are the best things one can buy with money. You don't need to compare the prices, no need to wait for the cheapest option to become available. Having a private jet was a luxury Mr Cabeza de Vaca could easily afford.

After reading my friend's letter, Mr Cabeza de Vaca had treated me like a king. If I had handed him the letter earlier, probably I would have saved myself a good beating. Anyway, it could have been much worse…

I had asked him about the content of the letter without obtaining a satisfactory reply. He avoided giving me a direct answer. When I insisted, he suddenly ended the conversation.

"Thank your friend in the other life. There's nothing else to say."

The only thing I had guessed, from the questions he had asked me after reading it, was that the mysterious letter said something about the Rock of the Missing. One of the things of my peculiar friend…

On the days that followed, while I recovered from the beating, I told him about our childhood adventures in Galicia. He asked repeatedly about all that, in particular about the Rock of the Missing. I explained to him all the events that had marked our lives forever, and, in particular, everything that had to do with the Rock. I told him about the village and its people: anecdotes and stories I knew. I liked to do it because it allowed me to remember many things I thought I had long forgotten. Once I started to pull the thread, one thing led to another and I strung together experiences and characters. He didn't tell me much; he preferred to listen rather than to talk. He did tell me the odd anecdote about his life, but they were very few. I remember those pleasant evenings, sitting on the porch of his house, drinking tequila and eating meat.

One day, he blurted out that we were going to the Rock of the Missing. I was totally dumbfounded; it was the last thing I would have expected in my life.

"We're leaving tomorrow; everything is ready. You're going to jump inside that *pinche* rock and it isn't a suggestion. It's an order. That's the condition for me to forgive your life. Otherwise, you'll have to pay for what your friend did… I don't care that you weren't responsible for it; somebody has to pay. However, this time the Rock will decide if you deserve to live or to die. To live and become a man able to face life with your head held high, or to die trying. I will accompany you there, to see what happens."

When we left, I felt really sorry for leaving that place. However weird it might seem, after several days there, I had become attached to that ranch.

I asked them for a few minutes to focus and pray. I took my wallet out. I extracted the envelope with the number 2 written on it. It was the second and last envelope my friend had given me for whenever my life was in danger. I opened it and started reading it. I knew it would be related to the Rock of the Missing. My friend was responsible for my being there now.

Dear friend:

If you're reading this it is because you opened envelope number 1 at the right moment. I didn't expect less from you. Now it's your turn to jump off the Rock of the Missing. You can do it. Remember my father's training: it's all down to psychology. Don't be afraid. The most important thing is to listen to the Dragon: follow the path of your heart. Follow that path and not the other one.

I tried to read the letter again, but the ink had bled with the rain.

What a shitty piece of advice! On the brink of death, with a jump that could cost me my life, with a high dive before me, and my friend had to carry on with his riddles. And on top of that, he overestimated me. Did he think I would understand his letter? Well, I didn't. Follow the path of your heart: that was what the Dragon had told me the night of the peyote. He'd spent the last moments of his life in a joke/game/riddle that was of no use. What a wanker. Or perhaps I was the wanker for wasting my time reading that instead of concentrating and getting ready before risking my life?

I crumpled the soaked piece of paper and threw it into the sea. It fell on the small well created at the bottom of the Rock of the Missing, right in the place where I had to jump.

Chapter 27. Don Prudencio

Don Prudencio was a fisherman; he'd been a fisherman all his life. He'd gone to Terranova with the cod fishing boats; later he had worked in Grand Sole; finally, in small coastal fishing vessels. A whole life at sea, from the first tides, that lasted months, to the last ones, that lasted hours. Getting progressively closer to the village and to his house; spending more time on dry land and less at sea but always with the sea as his loyal companion.

When he retired, he carried on fishing; it couldn't have been any other way. He had a small rowing boat – a barge – he took fishing every morning. He got up at four a.m. in the morning, rode on his old bicycle to the harbour and went fishing until midday. In the afternoon, after his nap, one could see him in his garage mending his fishing gear. So far, everything more or less normal: a hard life bound to the sea, like that of many others. What wasn't so normal and surprised everybody was his age. He was ninety-three! At ninety-three, he carried on getting up early, rowing, cycling, cooking… He did it all by himself!

His skin was the only thing that didn't contradict his age; it would be impossible to fit more wrinkles in that face, weathered by the saltpetre and the sun. However, his eyes wore a vivacious and intelligent expression. His hands, despite having the fingers twisted by arthritis, were strong like pliers. When he walked, his movements were rhythmic, those of somebody who's spent all his life balancing his body in the swaying sea.

After talking to Pirulo, I didn't know if I was more or less scared than before but I didn't want to think about it anymore. I had put the matter to rest. Pirulo wasn't as mad as he seemed – or at least not always, not all the time – but only my friend and I knew that; therefore, we were safe. If we hadn't managed to make him talk, the Guardia Civil would find it even more difficult. However, my friend had held on to a piece of advice from Pirulo I had already forgotten in the maelstrom of emotions: to go and talk to Don Prudencio. One afternoon, he came looking for me, as determined as ever.

"Let's go to see Don Prudencio."

"Don Prudencio?"

"Yes."

"What for?"

"Don't you remember that Pirulo told us to talk to him?"

"He said something; I don't remember what. Anyway, why should we pay attention to that madman? Didn't you say we shouldn't pay attention to him?"

"No. What I'm saying is that Pirulo has no credibility, and for that reason, we're not in danger no matter what he might tell people. A completely different matter would be for us to investigate a bit what he's told us. It could be the product of his madness or not; you've already noticed he isn't as lost to the world as they believe in the village."

"And what will we get from that?" I protested because I wanted to get all that mess out of my head.

"And what will we lose? I'm going to see him. You can do whatever you want but don't come to me later begging me to tell you about it."

I agreed, half-heartedly; I knew I'd be more anxious if I didn't go.

Located on the outskirts of the village, his house was unmistakable: it had vividly white walls, old roof tiles, and the windows, doors and the tiny balcony, painted in a vivid green. On the ground floor, there was a small garage. Its door was always half-open, with a chain and a padlock securing it. That was where he kept all his fishing gear: fishing rods, traps, some nets, a small outboard engine, hooks, oars, scoop nets, a landing net... It was a small big mess and the garage was precisely what gave its essence to the house.

A perennial smell of fish, petrol and saltpetre turned the house into a substitute ship. That smell was eclipsed, a couple of times a day, by the delicious homemade dishes Don Prudencio cooked. A simple dish of fresh fish and potatoes. The cats, attracted by the smell, were always prowling the area.

We turned up at his house at the perfect time – my friend had planned it well. We appeared right after his nap when he was sitting in his garage, smoking black tobacco and mending the nets.

"Good afternoon, Don Prudencio!" my friend greeted him, kindly.

"Good!"

"Can we sit down?"

"There, quiet!" he ordered us, pointing at one corner.

We sat down and stayed quiet, observing how he tied up the hooks to the fishing line. He was very dexterous.

"We talked to Pirulo a few days ago," my friend said, going straight to the point. "You're the one who knows the most things about him."

After a silent pause, so long that I thought he wouldn't bother answering us, finally he decided to talk.

"I have a lot of affection for José and I was also very good friends with his family."

"Pirulo's name is José?" I asked.

"No. José is called José. Now they call him Pirulo... And you? You aren't from here. Who are your parents?"

"My parents aren't from the village. We only come here during the summer holidays."

"Do you understand Galician?"

He had a very strong accent and I found it very difficult to understand him.

"Only a bit," I tried to say in Galician, to make myself more agreeable.

"I can't speak good Spanish. I worked with people who spoke it and I can speak it a bit but not well."

"I'm the grandson of Don Francisco, of the big house," my friend interrupted. "I believe my grandfather and you were good friends."

"You don't say! Don Francisco! I was very good friends with your grandfather," he exclaimed, looking fondly at my friend. "Don Francisco was a big and strong man. He could drag a barge along the beach with several girls inside. We used to challenge him at the parties. It's a shame what happened to him. Damn it! He was as good as he was big. He always helped me and never asked for anything in return. That was the type of man he was; that was his education. His family was rich, people with lots of money, but they always cared for others. That's never been forgotten. The father of your grandfather gave land to humble people. When there was hunger, he also gave food to people. That's how your family was; that's the kind of man your grandfather was."

"You're the oldest of the village; you know many interesting stories. We'd like you to tell us about José, whom people call Pirulo," my friend asked, politely.

While he carried on working, he started telling us the story.

"I've known José for a very long time; I was very friendly with his family. Fishermen from Santander, good people, they came to the village when José was already a young boy. The father was a funny man, always playing pranks and telling jokes. José was also a cheerful and clever boy. Everything went well until he fell madly in love with Iria, a young girl from a rich family. He was crazy for her and wrote love letters to her. To help him, I lent him several poetry books your father had given me," he said, addressing my friend: "Bécquer, Espronceda, Rosalía de Castro, Quevedo, etc."

"She was also in love with him. The problem was that Iria's family found out. They were stuck-up people, nouveau riche, better-than-thou kind of thing. In the end, they left the village; we weren't good enough for them. Not at all like your grandfather," he asserted, looking again at my friend. "What happened was that they didn't accept the relationship and the kids felt the floor had gone from under them. They carried on the contact, in secret, but the control was getting tougher. I carried on helping them as much as I could. Sometimes, I passed a poem to the girl from José. I was his accomplice." He smiled and winked. "With so many complications, they planned to run away, but it wasn't to be. Iria fell ill and died, nobody knows why. José, maddened by sorrow, wasn't even able to say goodbye. Not only did they not allow him to enter the house or go to the funeral, but they also blamed him for her illness. José did stupid things. He fell into abusing alcohol and drugs. He went astray for months and months but he didn't die because he was strong. His parents died, though. They couldn't bear seeing their son like that. That was the last straw for him…

"Then, I thought of a way to save him. I told him he could go on trial to decide if he deserved to live or not. A test that, if he survived it, he'd have no other option but to carry on living. What better test than the sea? Who'd be a better judge than our patron saint, the Lady of the Sea, who intercedes for her sons, the fishermen?"

"The Rock of the Missing," my friend interrupted.

"Yes." Don Prudencio seemed surprised. "The Rock of the Missing. Be it Our Lord or Lucifer whoever lived inside the entrails of the Rock, he'd get to decide about the life of the boy. If he didn't deserve to die, the Virgin would save him and he'd have to face the rest of his life. Dead or acquitted, either way, his suffering would end. I don't know if you have the slightest idea of how he was at the time, for me to come up with that suggestion…

"Once I told him that, his hope returned. His eyes shone for the first time in a long while. He didn't think about it twice; he went straight to the Rock of the Missing. I went with him to bear witness to the test. I didn't know if it would be a funeral or a christening, but I had the feeling that he'd be able to survive the trial. After so much suffering, he wouldn't get frightened by the lack of air. Suffering makes us hard; it makes us realise we can bear anything. And the tide was rising and the current would help him get out; he also had that on his side.

"He was so eager that he didn't hesitate at all: he jumped as he arrived. Those were the most fucked-up minutes of my life. It was really anxiety provoking. When I finally saw him, he was floating face down, passed out. I jumped into the water, dragged him out and tried to resuscitate him. For me, those moments were eternal and horrible; I was the one who pushed him to do it! Finally, I managed to get him breathing again.

"When he recovered, it wasn't him; it was your Pirulo. He went around confused, disoriented, uncoordinated, mad. Next day, he fell ill; he had a very high fever. He was delirious and shouted, talking about the Green Beings of the underwater cave. He was praying to the Virgin, screaming for her to help him. The fever disappeared, and most of the symptoms also improved in a few days, but the madness remained. He had moments of sanity when one could talk to him, but he disconnected again quickly and went back to his fantasy world. In one of those scarce moments of lucidity, he told me about his experience down there. It seems that, after diving for a stretch, when you've almost reached your limit, the cave divides into two. He chose the bad option on purpose, in order to die. He carried onwards. Then he saw some big green things and he can't remember anything else. The next thing was when he woke up after the fever, several days later.

"I didn't tell anybody in the village about the Rock of the Missing. The people saw his madness and assumed it was due to the drugs and the alcohol. It's possible they also helped, I don't know, but what really drove him mad was the Rock."

"No, Don Prudencio. What really drove him mad was the death of his girlfriend," my friend noted.

"I don't know. At my age, everything is relative. I've seen lots of people die. At first, I was very affected by it, then a bit less, and later hardly at all. Fathers, mothers, brothers, friends, nephews, neigh-bours, rich, poor... It reached a point when I was almost happy I wasn't the dead one. Now I'm not even happy; I count deaths the same way I count hooks: unfazed.

"Those were hard times when one fought with blood every day. When you held on to the rope of life with nails and teeth, even if the rope was covered in shit. Only the strongest and luckiest ones of us survived and that's not something to be sorry about, one should be thankful for it. The price one has to pay is to see those around you die. In the past, dying was the norm: children died of illnesses, mothers died at birth, men died at sea, even all together in the wars. Dead bodies and more dead bodies. I lived to work. Let's hope we always have enough work! We didn't ask for holidays, we didn't get bored, we weren't dissatisfied. We simply worked until we dropped, from sunup to sundown, because we were alive and we could. Am I going to complain, like the young ones do nowadays because I work too much? Because I don't have a car? Because I don't have holidays? Come on, man, come on! I'm an old codger who can't stop working. It's the same as when I go fishing on my boat: I row because I'm frightened that, if I stop rowing, we'll both sink. That's why I keep on rowing. And I can't abandon the only friend who doesn't die: the sea. She'll bury me as I did the rest. That's a comfort to me."

"I think I understand you," my friend said. "It's like the man who has a patch of tomatoes. He watches them grow and picks them up once and again. In the end, there's only the empty patch left, with no tomatoes. When a new spring comes, there are more tomatoes and more picking. In the end, you get used to them coming and going and nothing else, while you're the only thing that remains constant. You feel alone until you notice the oak tree at the bottom of the patch. That oak tree is also constant and will outlast you. It's the comfort of knowing you aren't alone and you'll have company when you die."

"Weeeell," Don Prudencio concluded. "Go home, there's rain coming."

"How do you know the rain is coming?" I asked.

"Because of the ants. Can you see all those flying ants coming out of the anthills? They come out when it's going to rain. Take notice, it never fails. And, the barges in the harbour are facing the sea, which means the wind is coming from there: bad weather for sure. This morning, the beach was full of seagulls, which only leave their cliffs when the weather is going to turn bad. You only need to pay attention to the sea, the wind and the animals. When you learn that, you don't need to listen to the radio. Who do you think warned people last time, when that yacht went missing? The old sailors, the only ones who know these things! We learned how important they were when we were little. Youths don't pay any attention; you believe watching the weather on television is enough. Then, things happen. Fucking hell!"

"Is there another big storm brewing?" I asked, a bit scared.

"Could be worse…"

When we left Don Prudencio's house, the storm seemed imminent. The air was charged; the static electricity made the atmosphere suffocating.

I was a bit dazed and angry. Now, I understood what Pirulo had told my friend. What I couldn't understand was why my friend had chosen the same option, if that was the option one chose to die – at least, according to Pirulo.

I told him, a bit cranky:

"You lied to me. You knew perfectly well what Pirulo was referring to when he talked about choosing the option of living or dying."

"I didn't want to talk about that the other day. It wasn't the right moment."

"Fuck, you could have told me. Now I understand your interest in talking to Don Prudencio. You aren't the only one who's gone in and out of the Rock of the Missing; you knew it."

"But I'm the only one who hasn't left his sanity inside. I gave it to the Green Beings and they gave it back to me. They didn't like it."

"It isn't funny. You don't take anything seriously, do you?"

"No."

"Not even your brother's death?"

As soon as I blurted it out, I regretted it. Although I was angry, it wasn't justified; I'd crossed the line. I hadn't meant to say that, but the unstoppable outburst of anger had broken the chains of a malice I was keeping prisoner inside.

He looked at me with hatred; he'd never looked at me that way before. It didn't last long; it was only a flash of lightning that illuminated his face for a few seconds.

"If I'm honest with you, not even that. I didn't kill him. He fell over by accident. I invented it the other

day to create an atmosphere. We had to inspire
Pirulo, to make him stop saying stupid things and
start being honest with us."

"You're sick. One shouldn't play with these kinds
of things," I replied, astonished by his confession.

"I'm not playing with it, I only shared what I felt
when it happened, and those feelings are true and
real. I didn't push him, but I felt as I said. It doesn't
matter if I pushed him or he fell down, I still feel
guilty about it. I am sorry for his death just the same.
It appears you are the one who is playing with it, the
one who uses it as a weapon. If it's such a serious
matter, why spit it in my face?"

I didn't know what to tell him. I was angry with
my friend, with myself, with everything that had
happened recently, even with the parents of Pirulo's
girlfriend. I was disgusted with the whole world.

We walked in silence until we went our separate
ways, without even saying goodbye.

The next day was the last one I spent in the village;
the holidays were coming to an end and we had to go
back. I was in a very bad mood; I didn't want to see
anybody, hence that morning I stayed at home. My
parents thought my bad mood was due to the end of
summer. After lunch, I left the house early and went
fishing alone; that way I could reflect on everything
and avoid my idiotic friend. What a stupid guy; I was
outraged at him for his lies and his nonsense. Because
of him, I did nothing but get into trouble and have a
hard time. On top of that, he only told me an infinites-
imal part of what happened, as if I were a tiny toddler
whom they only tell the minimum necessary. And he,

with that fucking calm of his, always above every-thing, laughing at everybody. 'Enough is enough! This ends here!' I thought. 'He can go and get others into trouble.'

I fished, talking to no one, cursing, annoyed as never before, and ruminating over my own indigna-tion. When the afternoon came to an end, I was on my way back home, lost in thought, and I didn't see him coming.

"Hi!" he greeted me, with a happy voice.

I didn't give him time for more, the rage inundated me and I threw a punch at his face with all my strength. He dropped to the floor. I simply left, full of myself, without looking back. Then, I locked myself at home and didn't want to go out. My parents noticed my bad mood and didn't ask many questions. I imagine they must have been surprised I didn't say goodbye to my friend that night.

Next day it was Sunday, and we got up very early. My parents liked to set off early to reach home by mid-afternoon.

The journey was terrible. The early start – we got up around six a.m. – turned my stomach. The smells bothered me: the car smelled of tobacco and petrol. And there were the twists and turns, especially at the beginning of the journey. All of that conspired to make me sick. We had to climb two mountain passes: Piedrafita and Manzanal. Once we'd overcome the bends and the mountain passes, we had to go through the horrific heat of the straight roads in Castile. The car wasn't air-conditioned and if my father opened his window a bit, it was still worse because the air was so dry and hot that it burned. With a T-shirt caught in the window, we tried to hide from the scorching sun, but it wasn't a very good solution. To sum it up, the journey – including some breaks – lasted around eleven hours and you had time to feel homesick for the summer, to reflect upon what had happened, and to think about your new plans with the city friends you hadn't seen in months.

I was quiet the whole journey, thinking. I felt terrible for having punched my friend. I didn't know if I had really hurt him. Would he have needed to see a doctor? Would he hate me and had I lost my friend?

'He deserved it,' I told myself to stir up my anger and to avoid feeling guilty. The problem was that my anger disappeared quickly and I felt regretful again.

I felt happy the summer was coming to an end and I was leaving the village. It was an anguished journey that replaced the usual melancholy of the return.

What I couldn't know then was that I wouldn't see my friend again for many years. It would be in Mexico, a place very far away from that Galician village of our childhood.

Chapter 28. Under the Rock

When you know you're going to die, you reach a state of calm, sober and solemn, where everything around you becomes important. Your senses sharpen and you can perceive things you normally wouldn't notice. It's as if you were trying to appreciate those last seconds, to remember everything, every detail, in a slow and special way.

It was raining slowly, everything was grey and there was a tremendous calm. I looked at the floor and saw some winged ants crawling out of a crack. I remembered Don Prudencio's words: a thunderstorm was coming.

Behind me, Cabeza de Vaca and his thugs were observing me, impatiently. I had to jump or they would kill me but if I jumped I'd probably die. I was scared.

I closed my eyes to concentrate. I could feel the waves breaking on the rock, the rain over my head, the smell of the sea and of the wet soil. I was cold wearing only my underwear. I had done that to make diving easier. Cabeza de Vaca had looked at me disapprovingly.

I started breathing deeply; I would need to accumulate a lot of air. I remembered my childhood, diving at the beach. I had my eyes closed and was trying not to think of anything but the images flashed through my head at full speed: the traps, Dark Shadow, the ghost yacht, Bad Quique, Pirulo, Don Prudencio and my friend. A lot of time had passed but it seemed as if it were only yesterday. I cursed my peculiar friend; I was here because of him.

I tried to think of something that would relax me and motivate me: an idea, a movie, a song. I remembered the scene where the protagonists of *Chariots of Fire* run through the beach, with the spectacular soundtrack as background. My mood improved and I calmed down somewhat. Then, the image of Paul Newman in *Cool Hand Luke* convinced he could eat fifty eggs, came to my head. I could do it.

I opened my eyes and looked down, at the spot I had to hit when I jumped. The height was enormous, the tide was very low. I realised we were in September, at the time of the *lagarteiras*, the strong tides. How long since I had thought about that...

'I must jump and pay my outstanding debt,' I thought.

I breathed air in for the last time; I filled up my lungs to the maximum and jumped into the abyss.

I fell with my feet first and sank into the water. I had hit right in the centre of the bottomless well, exactly where I had to fall to avoid smashing to bits on the rocks. I felt the current dragging me towards the bottom and I went deeper. The water was cold, although not as much as I expected – being cold before the jump hadn't been such a bad idea. The water of the cave wasn't muddy and there was more water than I expected; I could see reasonably well. I kept moving forward and I was surprised that the tunnel, instead of becoming narrower, was getting wider. I still had plenty of air left; I was feeling calm.

I reached a junction. The underwater cave split into two arms: the right one went up, the left one, down. I thought I couldn't afford a second's hesitation; I had to choose straight away. I wanted to choose the right one because it went up. My friend's letter said: 'The most important thing is to listen to the Dragon: follow the path of your heart. Follow that path and not the other one.' I tried to remember something else from my childhood. Pirulo and my friend had talked about it, but they never said which option should be chosen.

I had hardly any air left. My heart told me to go up. I had to decide immediately. I thought Bad Quique might have died because he hesitated for too long; it was as dangerous to doubt as it was to make the wrong choice.

The right one! I chose the right path, the one that went up. I swam with strong strokes. The path narrowed and got darker, but it went up and up. I had chosen correctly!

I reached the last stretch quite composed. The feeling of having chosen correctly gave me extra motivation and strength. The tunnel narrowed even more and I saw it ended in a small hole. I went through it and entered a wide and round cave. As soon as I entered it I saw a skull. Fuck, a skull! A skull!

Then I saw it clearly: the left side is where the heart is. It wasn't the right arm the one I should have chosen! It wasn't the one that went up! Although it went down, the correct one was the left one. I had made a mistake. My God, I'd made a mistake! That mistake would cost me my life! The anguish consumed the last of my air. I went to turn around but realised it would be a waste of time. I didn't have enough air to go back; in fact, I had no air left at all. With a final push, I reached the centre of the cavity where I was. There was a bit of light and I saw that the place was full of bones and skulls. There were skeletons all over the place!

'A bit of light,' I thought. 'I can see a bit of light! Perhaps there is a way out.' With no energy left, I got closer to the point where the light came from. It was at the end, in the highest part of the cave where I was. There was a minuscule aperture, but there was no exit. I tried to push because the surface was right there. I couldn't. The dice had rolled: I was going to drown. However, when I pushed with my hand I noticed there was a small area containing air. The tide was so low it had left that small part uncovered. I held on to a protrusion from the rock and stuck my face eagerly to the wall, scratching my cheek on the rocks but I felt no pain: the freedom I experienced when the air entered my lungs eclipsed everything. I stayed there, quiet, breathing with difficulty, thinking, and recovering. When Bad Quique had jumped, it hadn't been in September, the tide wasn't as low and he didn't have access to the reservoir of air. He must have gone back; otherwise, the tide wouldn't have managed to get him out of the cave for me to find him where I did. If he hadn't tried to return, he'd be there, dead, missing, like the rest of the bodies in the underwater cave. Bad Quique was brave and strong because once you've reached the end and realised you have no way out, you have to be pretty strong-minded to try to go back. There, at the bottom of the cave, crouching and stuck to the ceiling like glue to breathe, I felt respect for that bully from my childhood. In the end, he'd proven he had a good pair of balls; he didn't give up easily like the skulls there. He must have swum almost up to the exit.

I heard the speedboat. Then, I thought about my situation again; I had become another missing man, another legend of the Rock. The Mexicans were going back to their country; they'd given me up for dead. The worse thing was that I might prove them right yet. I was alive, but I hadn't managed to come out of the cave.

The noise of the propeller disappeared in the distance. They'd gone! I was sure they didn't want to stay there any longer to avoid getting into any trouble. I waited a bit more. The position was very uncomfortable, I was very cold and the water was starting to rise; I had to get out of the cave straight away. Again, I tried to relax and breathe deeply. I accumulated as much air as I could and set off on my way back. I left the cave with the skulls, traversed the tunnel swimming with big strokes and reached the junction. My head was telling me to go back the way I'd come in. I knew the way and I knew what it was like. The other tunnel went down, that was why Pirulo had chosen it to die. However, it must have an exit: my friend had chosen it to live…

I didn't hesitate even half a second. Follow the path of your heart. My heart was telling me I had to do it. Ten years living in fear were too many. A decade with a question hanging over me was too long. I propelled myself hard towards the unknown path; the current was in my favour. That was what my friend must have noticed, that was why he'd chosen that way. The current was stronger in that part of the cave and I held on to the idea that it must have an exit. I advanced forward, with all the energy I could, submerging myself more and more on following the descending route of the cave. It was very long, much more than I had expected, and the light didn't reach this part; it was almost completely dark. Not being able to see, I became a bit disoriented and thought I had carried on descending. I couldn't go back. The air was almost depleted. I had kept a small reserve, but there was hardly any left. Finally, I saw a light again; it looked like the hoped-for way out. While I pushed myself with both hands, holding on to the edges of the exit hole, I let go of the little air I had left in my lungs.

I was outside the cave, but still under water. I looked up, agitated: I had a good distance to go to reach the surface. I had to keep going a few metres longer, a few seconds more. I closed my eyes and moved my legs slowly, without sudden movements. I kept my arms glued to my body; I had no air left to move them. I felt how the blood pulsed hard in my temples. I couldn't hold on any longer. 'Another instant, hold on just another instant, don't lose consciousness,' I told myself. Then, finally, I reached the long-awaited surface and breathed in, desperately. My lungs filled. I was so exhausted that I floated on my back to catch my breath. The rain was falling on me and the waves rocked me hard. I was alive, more alive than ever. I had managed without any help. I had done it! After enjoying the moment, I remembered I had my clothes at the Rock of the Missing. I looked and there was nobody there. Yes, Cabeza de Vaca and his Mexican thugs had gone. I swam calmly to the rock and climbed to the top. My clothes weren't there. They had taken them to avoid leaving any evidence behind. Resignedly, I swam slowly to the beach of the Drowned. I was in no hurry; nobody in the whole world knew I was here, nobody was waiting for me. I was missing. I was free.

Once at the beach, I collapsed on the sand. The rain was getting stronger. I must have looked like a madman: soaked, wearing only my underwear and with my eyes burning from the salty water. I took my time. The rain was life and I was feeling good. I felt in harmony with nature, at peace with the sea and with God. My life had been pardoned. After a while, I'm not sure exactly how long, I got ready to climb the steep slope up to the small cove. I reached the top slowly, calmly. I was so drenched that there was no point in rushing or trying to find shelter. I set off through the forest that would take me back to the village. It smelled strongly of eucalyptus and wet soil. In the middle of the narrow path, I saw somebody waiting for me.

It was Pirulo! Good old Pirulo looked exactly the same as usual. He hadn't changed or grown older at all. I approached him, happy, and hugged him. He hugged me back.

"I saw you do it. I don't understand it. I saw you go in and out. You couldn't survive that long without breathing. The Green Beings must have helped you. Now you're a Green. Come with me."

I followed him across the forest. We left the path and started walking through the fields. We climbed to the top of the mountain. The ferns made walking difficult and the slope was very steep, but I was very fit. Finally, we reached a cave. The entry was covered in ferns. Unless you knew its exact position, it was impossible to find. It was Pirulo's house, his enigmatic hideout that nobody had ever discovered. Now I knew where it was.

There wasn't much there: a mattress with a thick blanket, several cartons of wine, numerous climbing ropes to use to catch barnacles and a cylinder with petrol. No evidence of the motorbike.

He lent me some dry clothes. They almost fitted me; I had lost a lot of weight. The thunderstorm outside was very violent: we could hear the wind howling through the trees and the continuous cracking of the eucalyptus moaning about the attack of the tempest. I started to feel cold; it was very humid in the cave. He offered me wine and we drank it. We didn't talk, it wasn't necessary; we were both survivors of the Rock of the Missing. He had his Green Beings and I had my Dragon; we were more alike than I'd ever imagined. What a pair of madmen! Although thinking about it, in the state he'd found me – soaked and only wearing my underwear – I must have seemed still crazier than Pirulo. To be next to Pirulo and seem crazier than him wasn't without merit... I started laughing; those kinds of thoughts were typical of my friend. I laughed even more and Pirulo joined me, laughing too. We laughed together for a good while. We drank a toast to my friend solemnly, we clinked our wine cartons vehemently. I raised my little finger when I drank, again in honour of my friend. We laughed again and drank, laughed and drank.

I woke up due to the light entering the cave. I was alone. Pirulo had left. When I went out, I saw the storm had ended; a wonderful morning, with a fresh atmosphere and a shining sun, welcomed my new life. I lay on a rock, like a lizard, and allowed the sun to warm me. I closed my eyes and felt an enormous wellbeing; I didn't want to move from there, I was in no hurry. After a good while, Pirulo turned up and I felt so happy to see him that I hugged him, affectionately. He tensed up; he didn't appreciate that morning's outpouring of emotions too much. I asked him to lend me a bit of money and swore I'd give it back.

"You don't need to give me anything back," he replied as he gave it to me.

I took the bus to Ferrol. People looked at me. I looked like a picture! When I finally reached the train station, I went straight to the ticket office.

"A ticket to Madrid, please. The cheapest you have."

"Check the timetable for prices and times," the person who sold them replied, quite unpleasantly.

"Couldn't you give me any guidance? Which one leaves first?"

"Haven't you heard me? Check the timetable for prices and times."

"Could you lend me a pen to write it down?" I asked him, very kindly, pointing at the one he had on the counter.

My train left that night. The money Pirulo had given me didn't stretch much, and the ticket was third class. In third class, there were no berths, and I would have to sit up all night in a tiny cubicle with five other people.

I got on the train slowly. I'd learned not to be in a hurry, to take life calmly. I looked at my travelling companions and sat in the only place left. I did it without any concerns, but also decisively and firmly.

There were several peculiar individuals, but the most peculiar of them all was the one sitting right next to me. Was it because nobody wanted to sit next to him or was it fate? After all, I attracted weird people... I put my hand in my pocket and touched the pen. I smiled. I had a long journey ahead of me and I wasn't scared or anxious. Now I was ready and the journey – life – seemed to me a fascinating and funny adventure.

The weird guy sitting next to me started talking to me. I sensed some dark madness in his eyes and, instead of worrying or becoming upset, I was interested. I didn't feel shy or need to resort to anger or fury to overcome my insecurities.

He talked in Galician with a strong accent.

"Boy, grab your money and let's go have a drink. They told me the train has a canteen."

"I have no money, my friend," I replied, calmly and kindly. "I'm truly sorry. If I did, I'd invite you to some wine and a bite of pumpernickel and cheese."

"Thanks, my friend," he replied, resignedly.

"Do you know something?" I asked him. "Travelling by train is wonderful. Don't you think travelling in third class is like the owner of a tomato patch...?"

Acknowledgements

To Carol and my children: they are the best that has happened to me in my life. To my parents, my brother and my aunt Piti; they'll always be in my heart.

To all who, apart from those previously mentioned, have read the novel and given me their support, ideas and corrections: Margarita, Uncle Manolo, Jander, Julián, Isa, Juan F., Patricia, Ida, Jean, Ana and Ramón.

A special mention goes to Ildefonso, for his help with the Mexican dialogues, and to Xulio, together with my friends from Lugo, for their lessons in Galician. Any mistakes are my own.

With reference to the cover, I've worked two very good friends to exhaustion. Oscar created the first cover for my first book; I'll never forget it. The current one is by Javier, a true phenomenon.

Dear Reader:

You can get in touch with me to share your comments, reviews, questions and suggestions.

E-mail:

therockofthemissing@gmail.com

Facebook:

The Rock of the Missing